LUKE PEARSON

HILDA
AND
THE BIRD
PARADE

FLYING EYE BOOKS

LONDON - LOS ANGELES

THIS PAPERBACK EDITION PUBLISHED IN 2016 BY FLYING EYE BOOKS,
AN IMPRINT OF NOBROW LTD, 27 WESTGATE STREET, LONDON, E8 3RL.

6 8 10 9 7

PUBLISHED IN THE US BY NOBROW (US) INC
PRINTED IN POLAND ON FSC® CERTIFIED PAPER

ISBN: 978-1-911171-02-7

MIX
Paper from responsible sources
FSC® C163799

WWW.FLYINGEYEBOOKS.COM

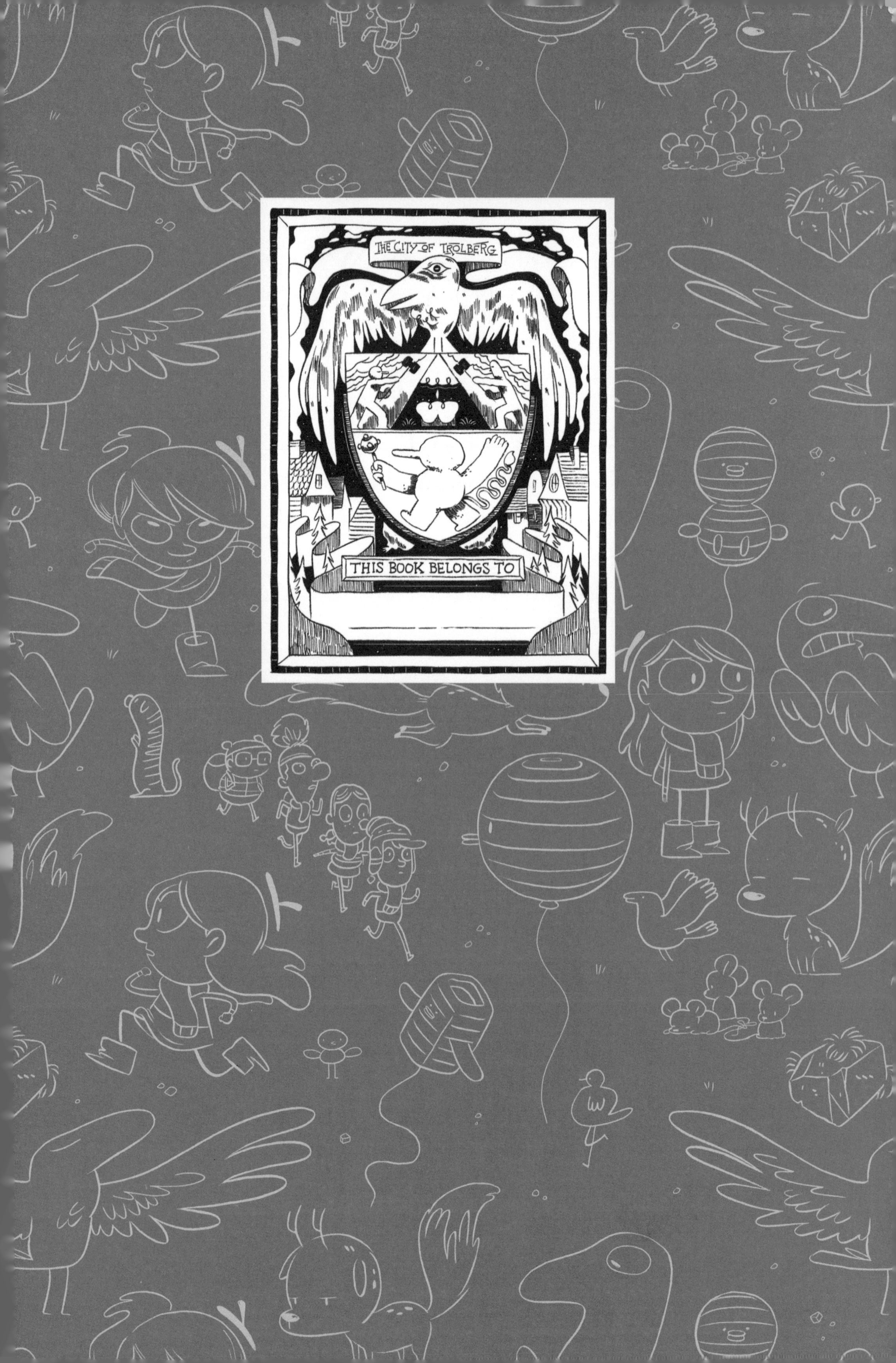
THE CITY OF TROLBERG
THIS BOOK BELONGS TO

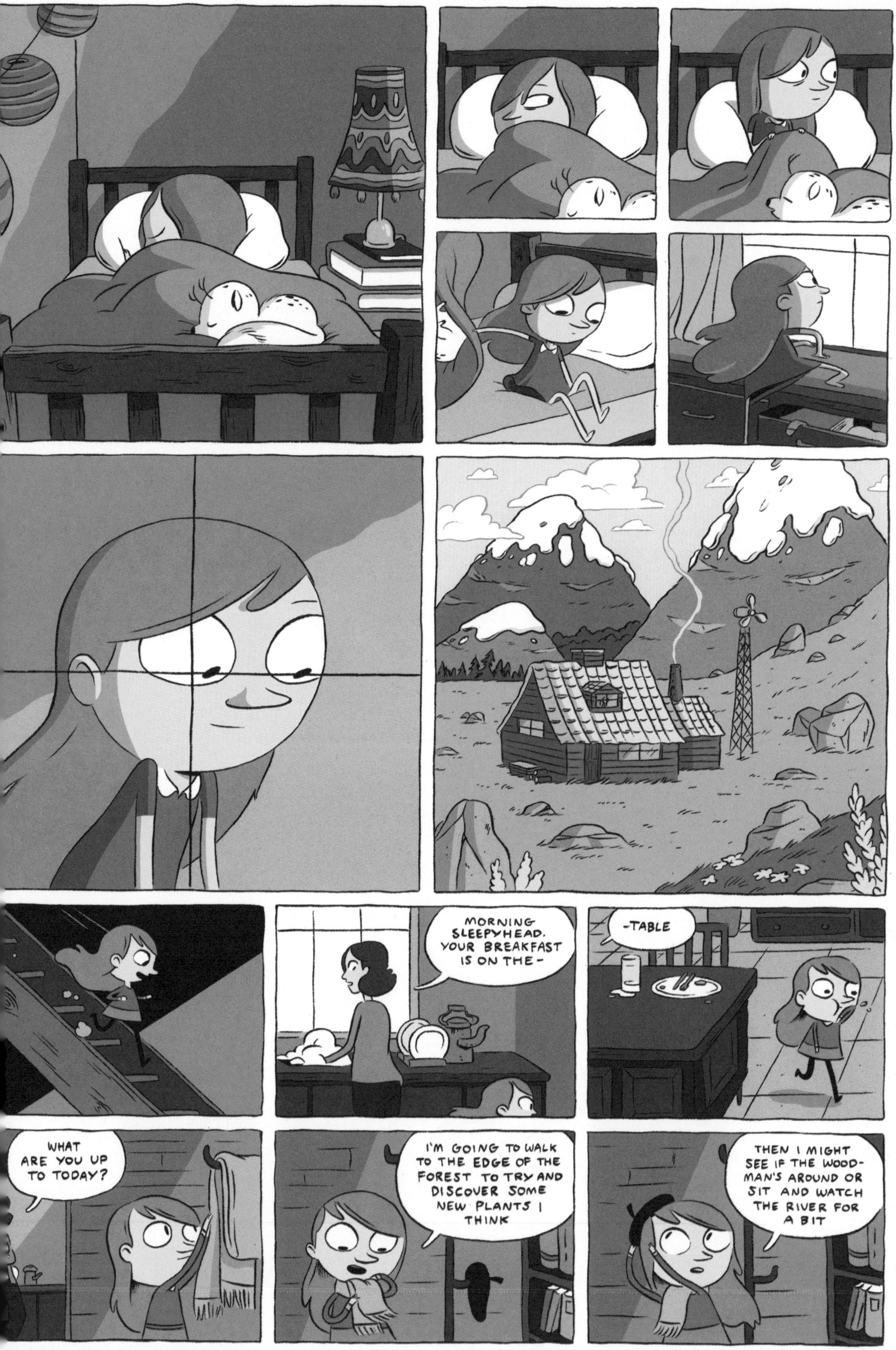
MORNING SLEEPYHEAD. YOUR BREAKFAST IS ON THE-
-TABLE
WHAT ARE YOU UP TO TODAY?
I'M GOING TO WALK TO THE EDGE OF THE FOREST TO TRY AND DISCOVER SOME NEW PLANTS I THINK
THEN I MIGHT SEE IF THE WOOD-MAN'S AROUND OR SIT AND WATCH THE RIVER FOR A BIT

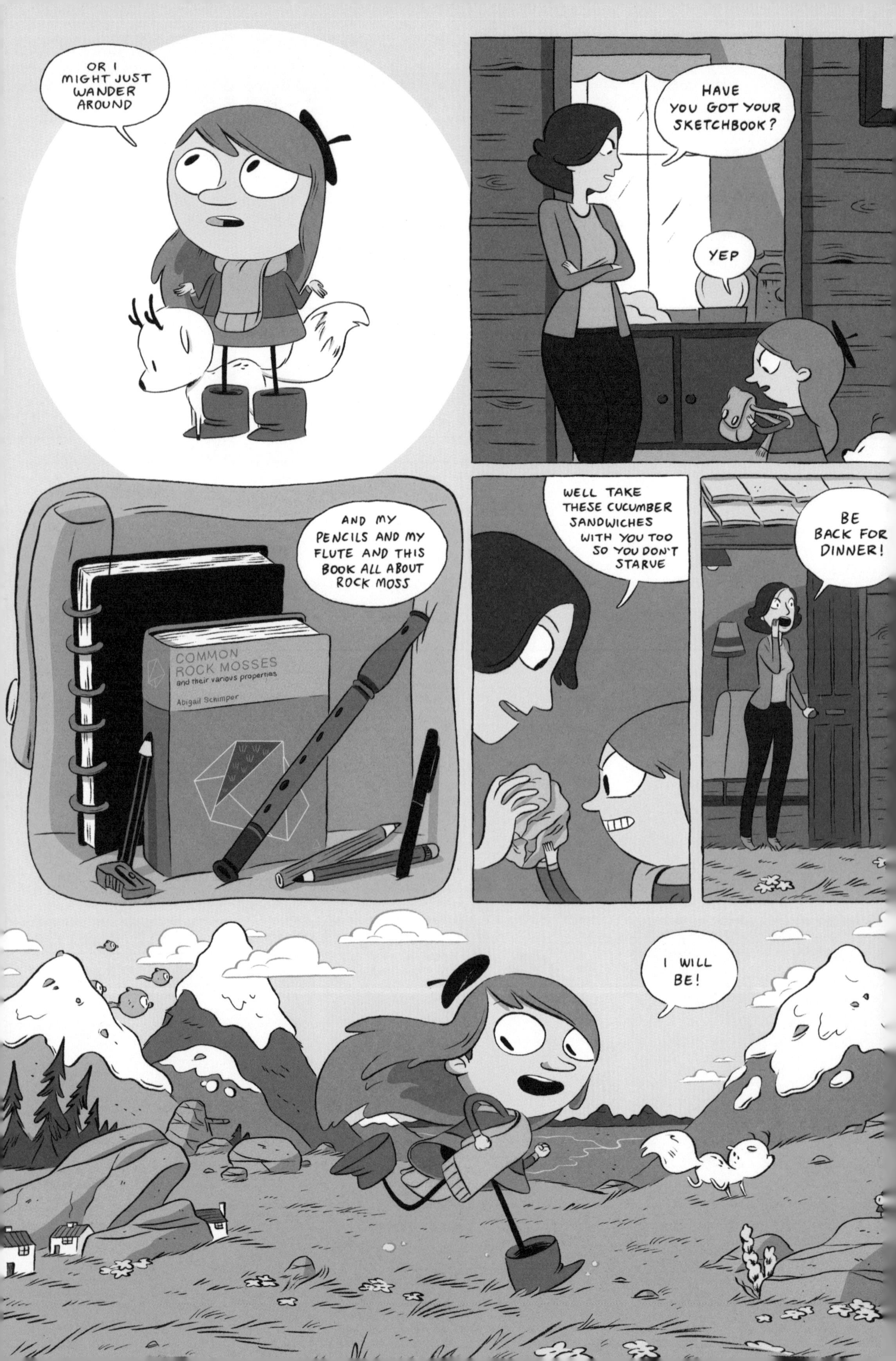
OR I MIGHT JUST WANDER AROUND
HAVE YOU GOT YOUR SKETCHBOOK?
YEP
AND MY PENCILS AND MY FLUTE AND THIS BOOK ALL ABOUT ROCK MOSS
COMMON ROCK MOSSES and their various properties
Abigail Schimper
WELL TAKE THESE CUCUMBER SANDWICHES WITH YOU TOO SO YOU DON'T STARVE
BE BACK FOR DINNER!
I WILL BE!

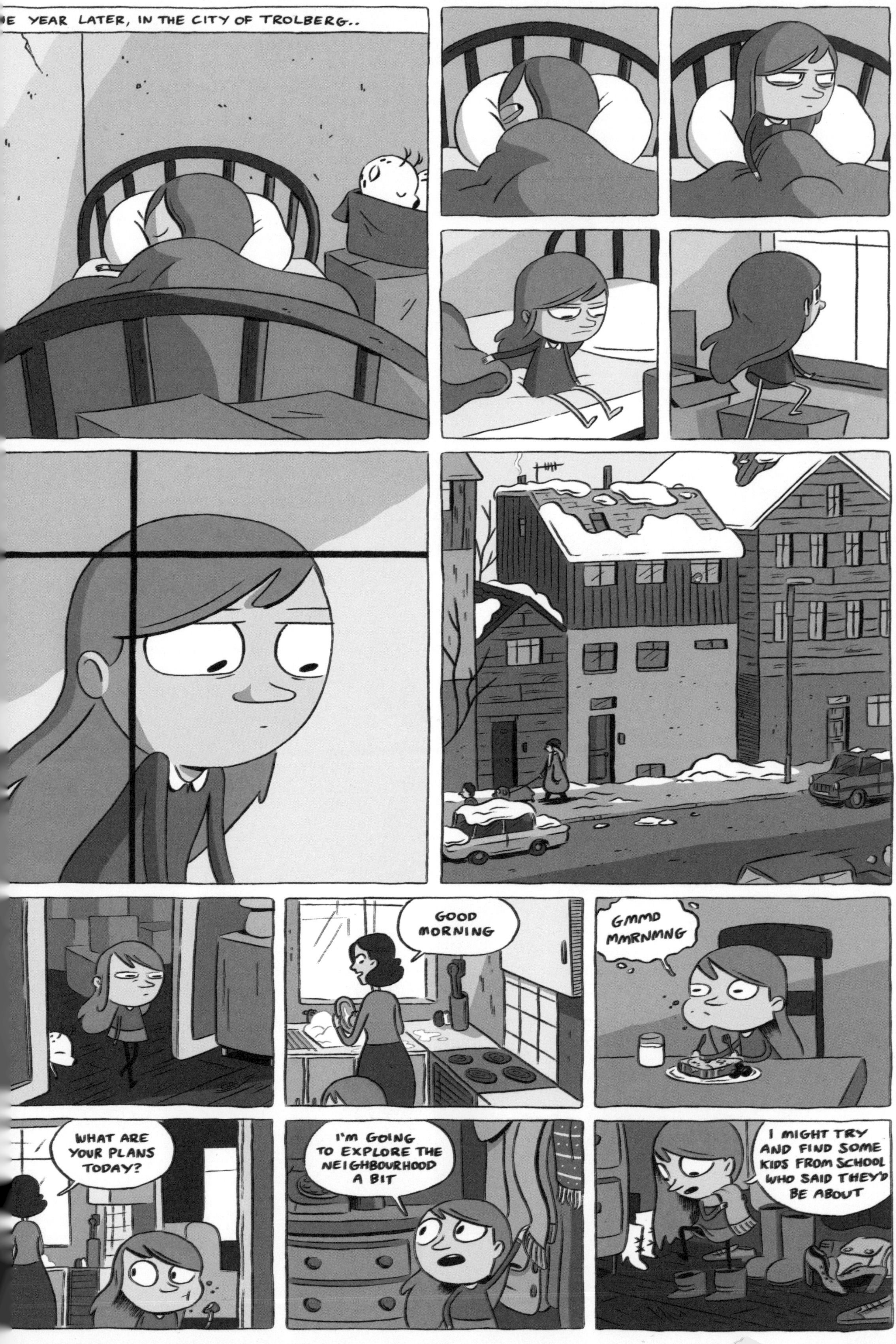
E YEAR LATER, IN THE CITY OF TROLBERG..
GOOD MORNING
GMMD MMRNMNG
WHAT ARE YOUR PLANS TODAY?
I'M GOING TO EXPLORE THE NEIGHBOURHOOD A BIT
I MIGHT TRY AND FIND SOME KIDS FROM SCHOOL WHO SAID THEY'D BE ABOUT

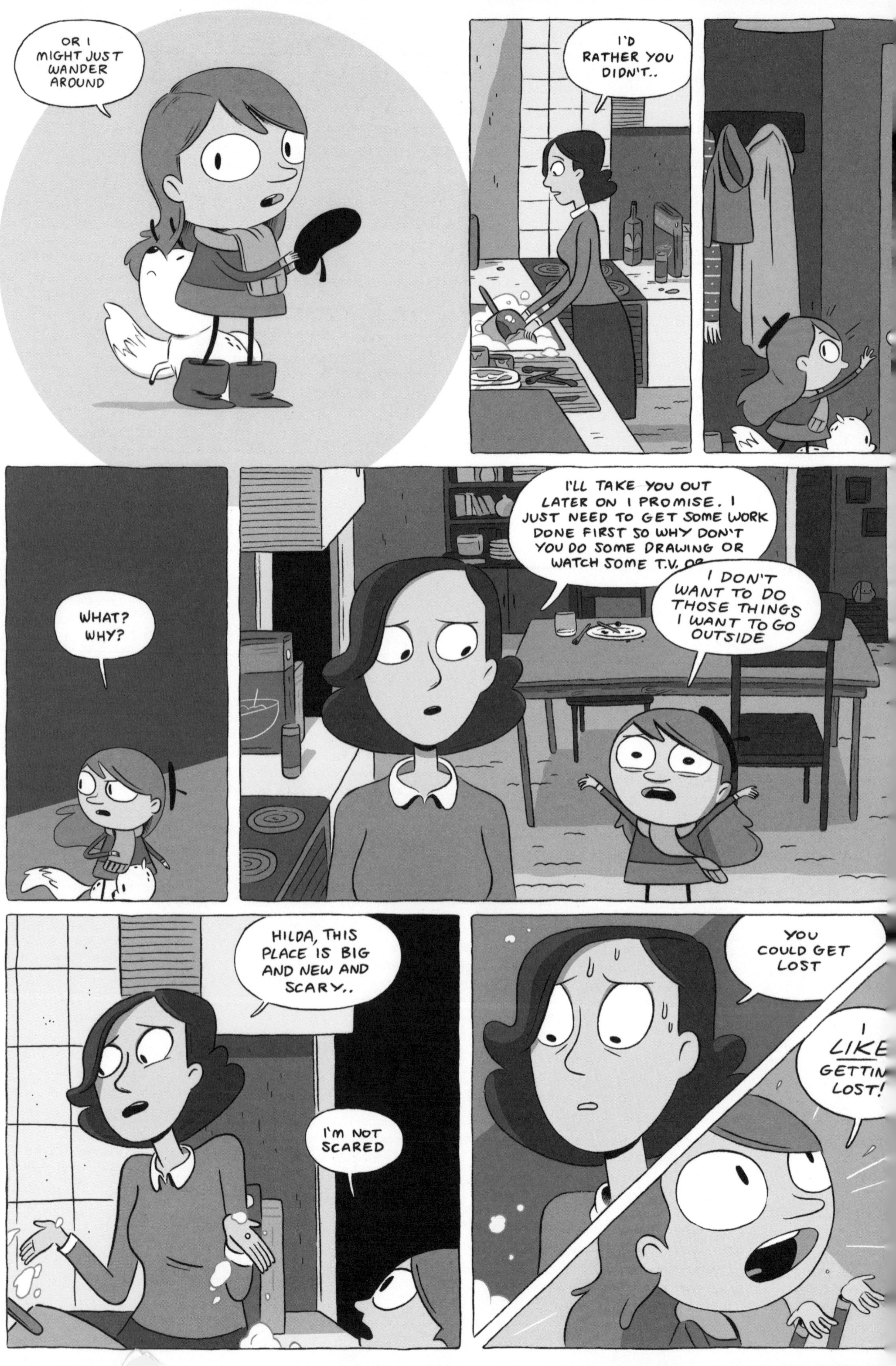
OR I MIGHT JUST WANDER AROUND
I'D RATHER YOU DIDN'T..
WHAT? WHY?
I'LL TAKE YOU OUT LATER ON I PROMISE. I JUST NEED TO GET SOME WORK DONE FIRST SO WHY DON'T YOU DO SOME DRAWING OR WATCH SOME T.V.
I DON'T WANT TO DO THOSE THINGS I WANT TO GO OUTSIDE
HILDA, THIS PLACE IS BIG AND NEW AND SCARY..
I'M NOT SCARED
YOU COULD GET LOST

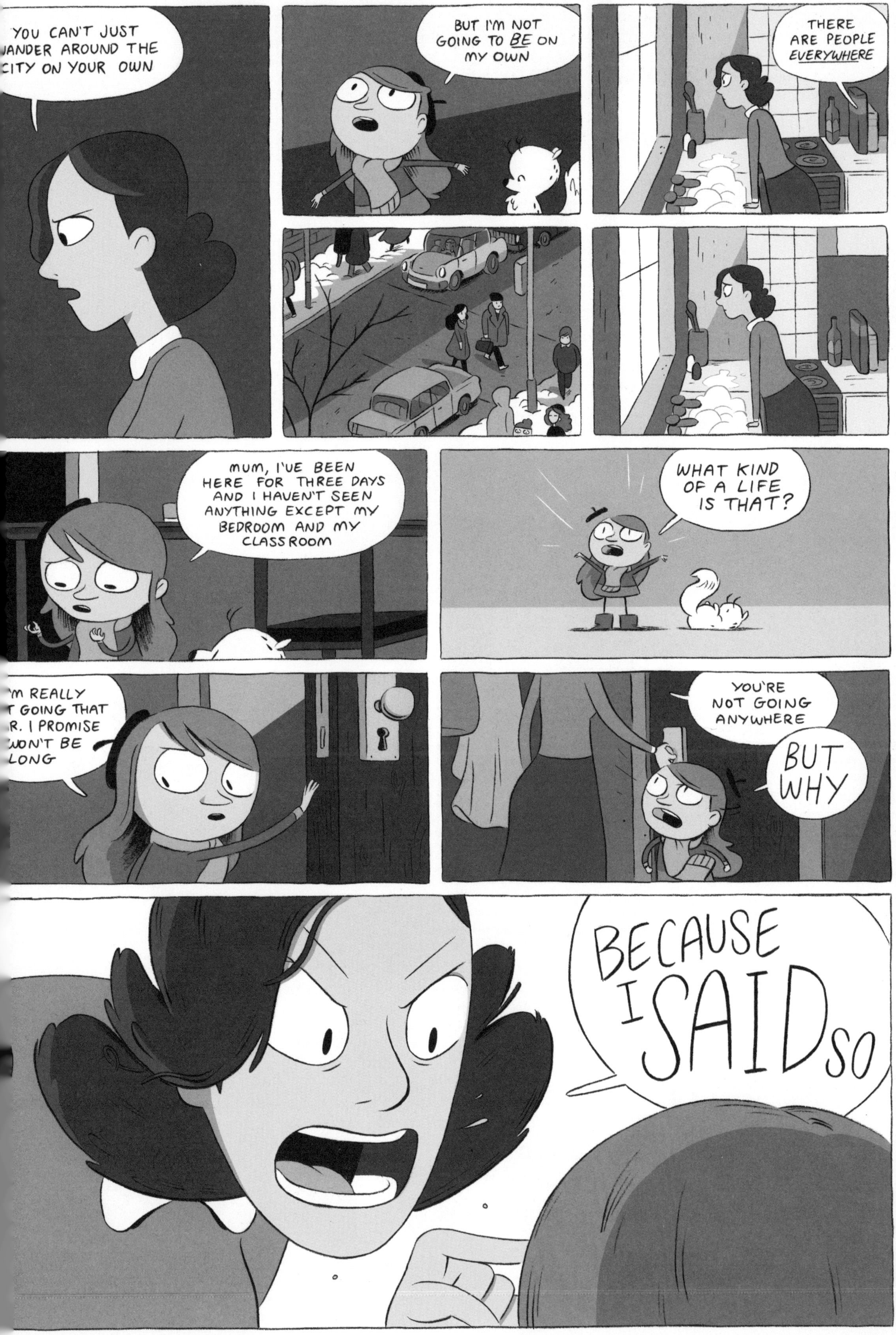

YOU CAN'T JUST ANDER AROUND THE CITY ON YOUR OWN
BUT I'M NOT GOING TO BE ON MY OWN
THERE ARE PEOPLE EVERYWHERE
MUM, I'VE BEEN HERE FOR THREE DAYS AND I HAVEN'T SEEN ANYTHING EXCEPT MY BEDROOM AND MY CLASSROOM
WHAT KIND OF A LIFE IS THAT?
M REALLY T GOING THAT R. I PROMISE WON'T BE LONG
YOU'RE NOT GOING ANYWHERE
BUT WHY
BECAUSE I SAID SO

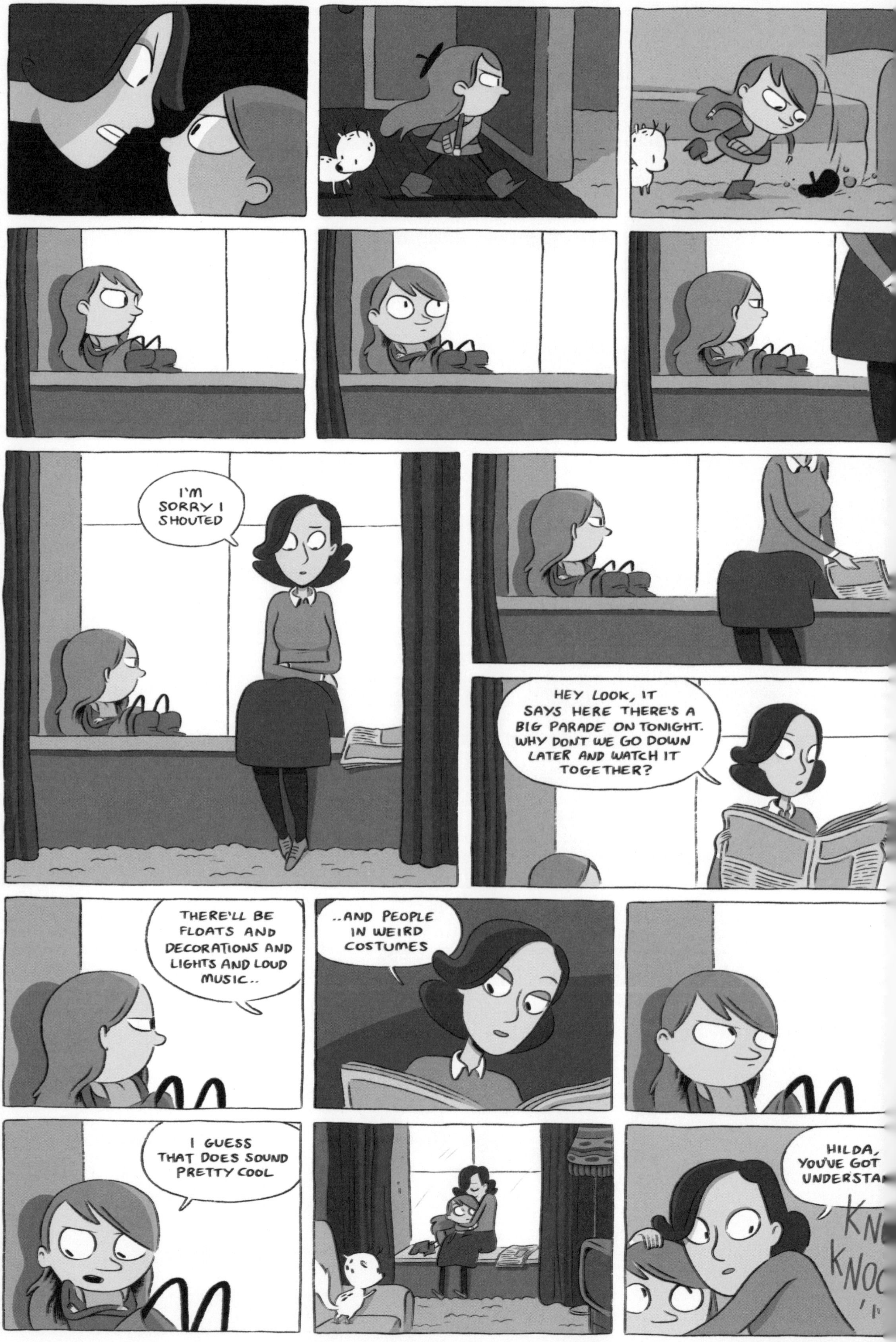
I'M SORRY I SHOUTED
HEY LOOK, IT SAYS HERE THERE'S A BIG PARADE ON TONIGHT. WHY DON'T WE GO DOWN LATER AND WATCH IT TOGETHER?
THERE'LL BE FLOATS AND DECORATIONS AND LIGHTS AND LOUD MUSIC..
..AND PEOPLE IN WEIRD COSTUMES
I GUESS THAT DOES SOUND PRETTY COOL
HILDA, YOU'VE GOT
UNDERSTA
KN
KNOC

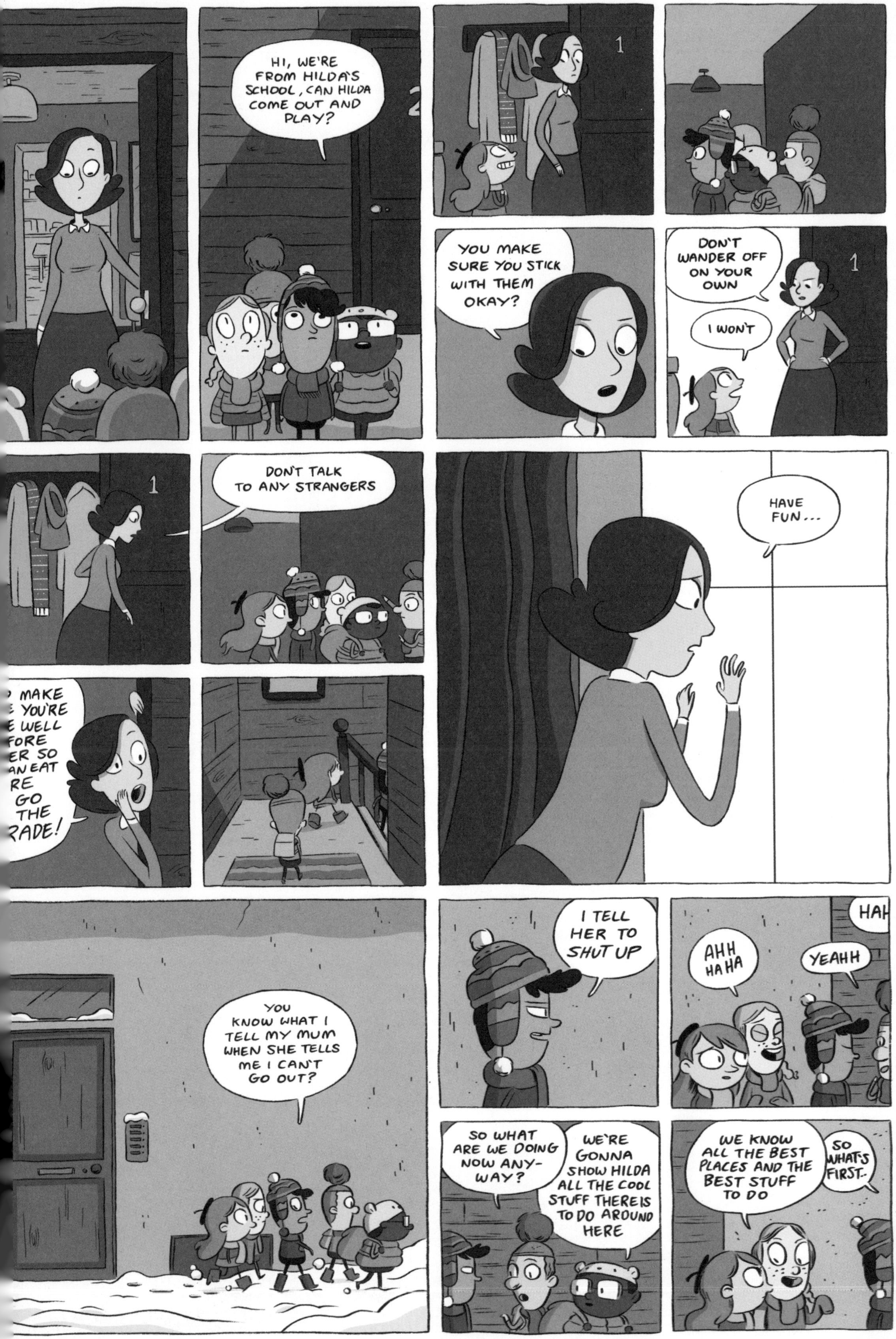

HI, WE'RE FROM HILDA'S SCHOOL, CAN HILDA COME OUT AND PLAY?
1
YOU MAKE SURE YOU STICK WITH THEM OKAY?
DON'T WANDER OFF ON YOUR OWN
I WON'T
1
DON'T TALK TO ANY STRANGERS
HAVE FUN...
MAKE YOU'RE WELL FORE ER SO AN EAT RE GO THE RADE!
YOU KNOW WHAT I TELL MY MUM WHEN SHE TELLS ME I CAN'T GO OUT?
I TELL HER TO SHUT UP
AHH HAHA
YEAHH
HAH
SO WHAT ARE WE DOING NOW ANY-WAY?
WE'RE GONNA SHOW HILDA ALL THE COOL STUFF THERE IS TO DO AROUND HERE
WE KNOW ALL THE BEST PLACES AND THE BEST STUFF TO DO
SO WHAT'S FIRST.

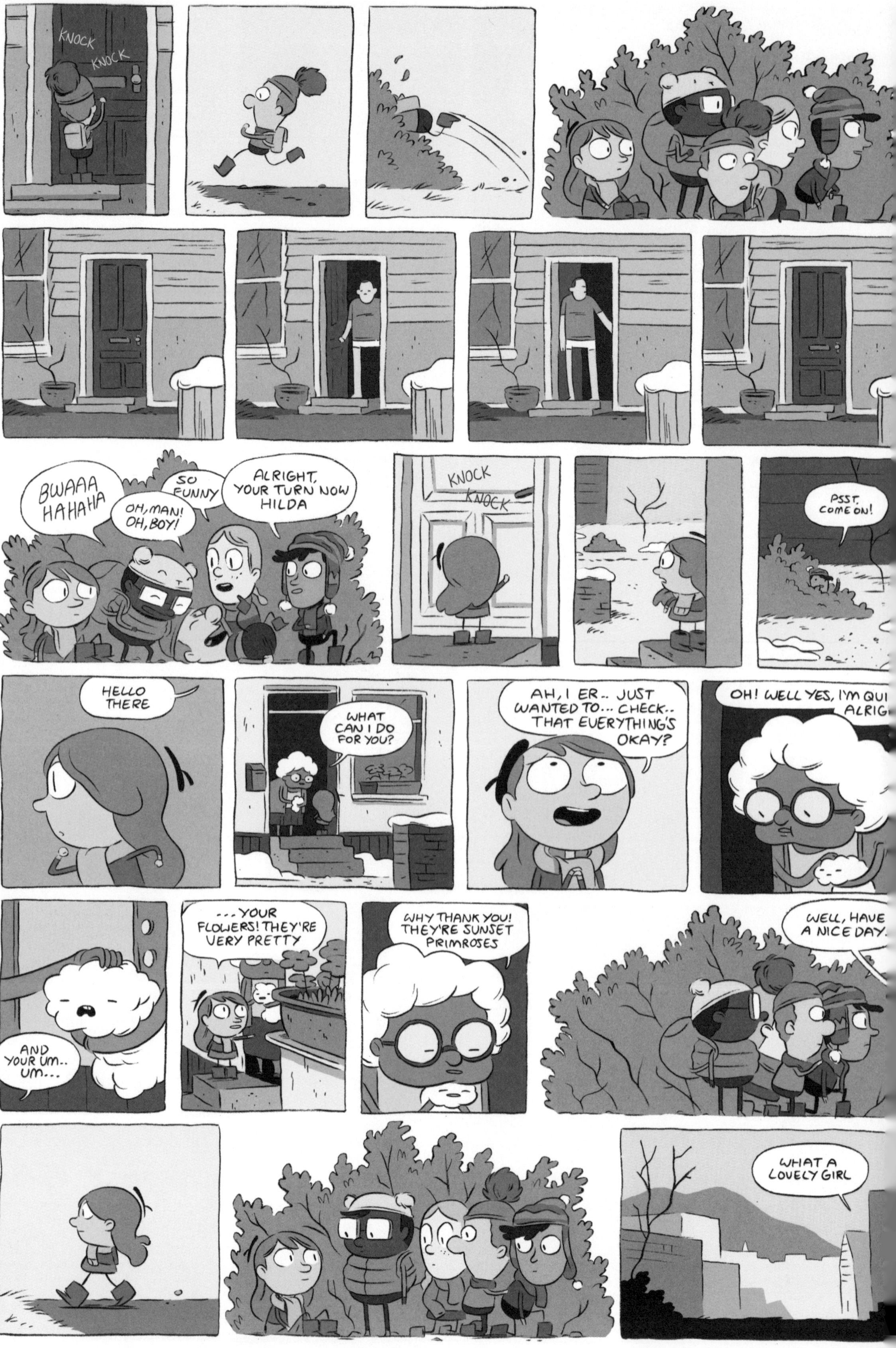
KNOCK
KNOCK
BWAAA HAHAHA
OH, MAN! OH, BOY!
SO FUNNY
ALRIGHT, YOUR TURN NOW HILDA
KNOCK
KNOCK
PSST. COME ON!
HELLO THERE
WHAT CAN I DO FOR YOU?
AH, I ER.. JUST WANTED TO... CHECK.. THAT EVERYTHING'S OKAY?
OH! WELL YES, I'M QUI
ALRIG
AND YOUR UM.. UM...
...YOUR FLOWERS! THEY'RE VERY PRETTY
WHY THANK YOU! THEY'RE SUNSET PRIMROSES
WELL, HAVE A NICE DAY.
WHAT A LOVELY GIRL

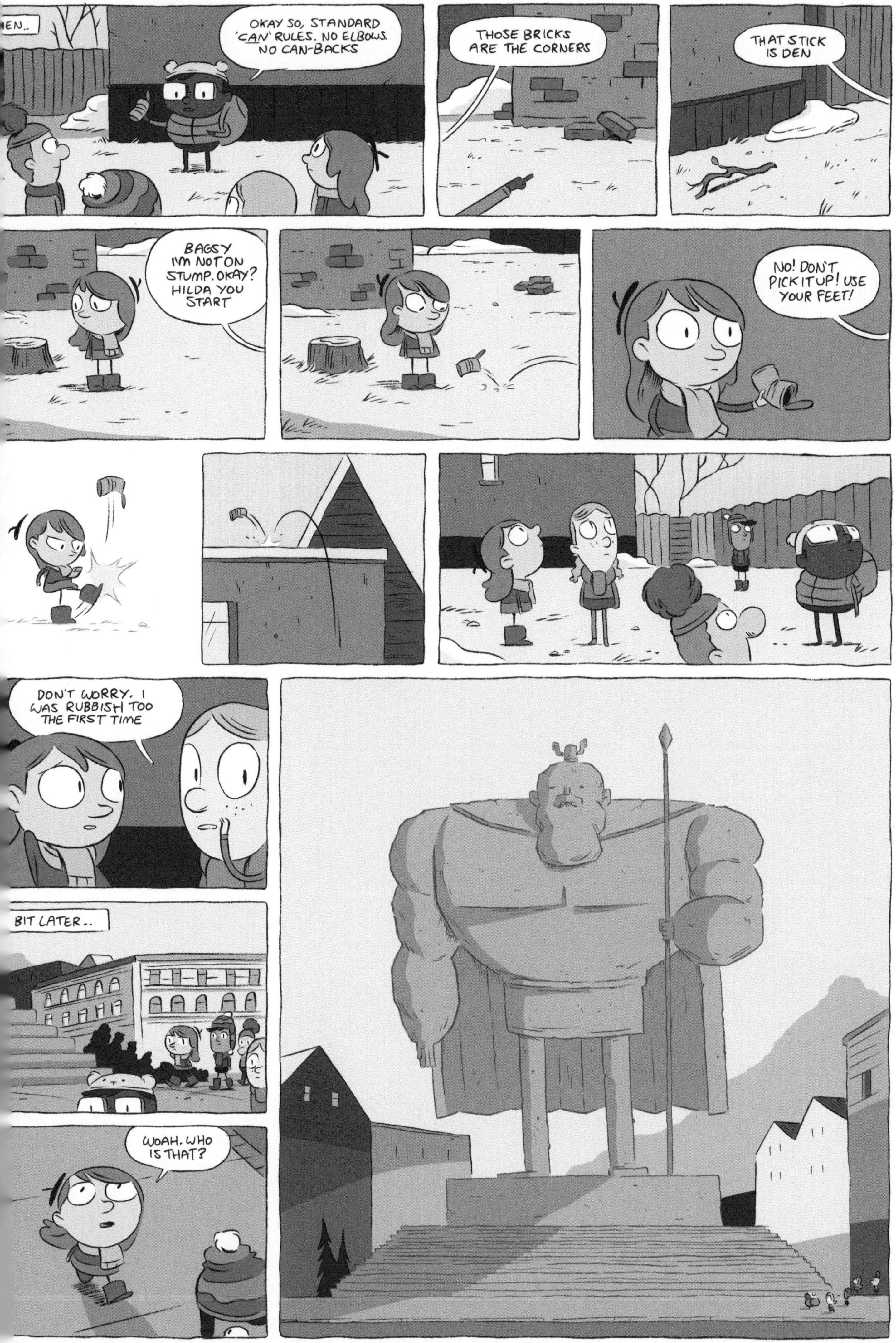
EN..
OKAY SO, STANDARD 'CAN' RULES. NO ELBOWS. NO CAN-BACKS
THOSE BRICKS ARE THE CORNERS
THAT STICK IS DEN
BAGSY I'M NOT ON STUMP. OKAY? HILDA YOU START
NO! DON'T PICK IT UP! USE YOUR FEET!
DON'T WORRY. I WAS RUBBISH TOO THE FIRST TIME
BIT LATER..
WOAH. WHO IS THAT?

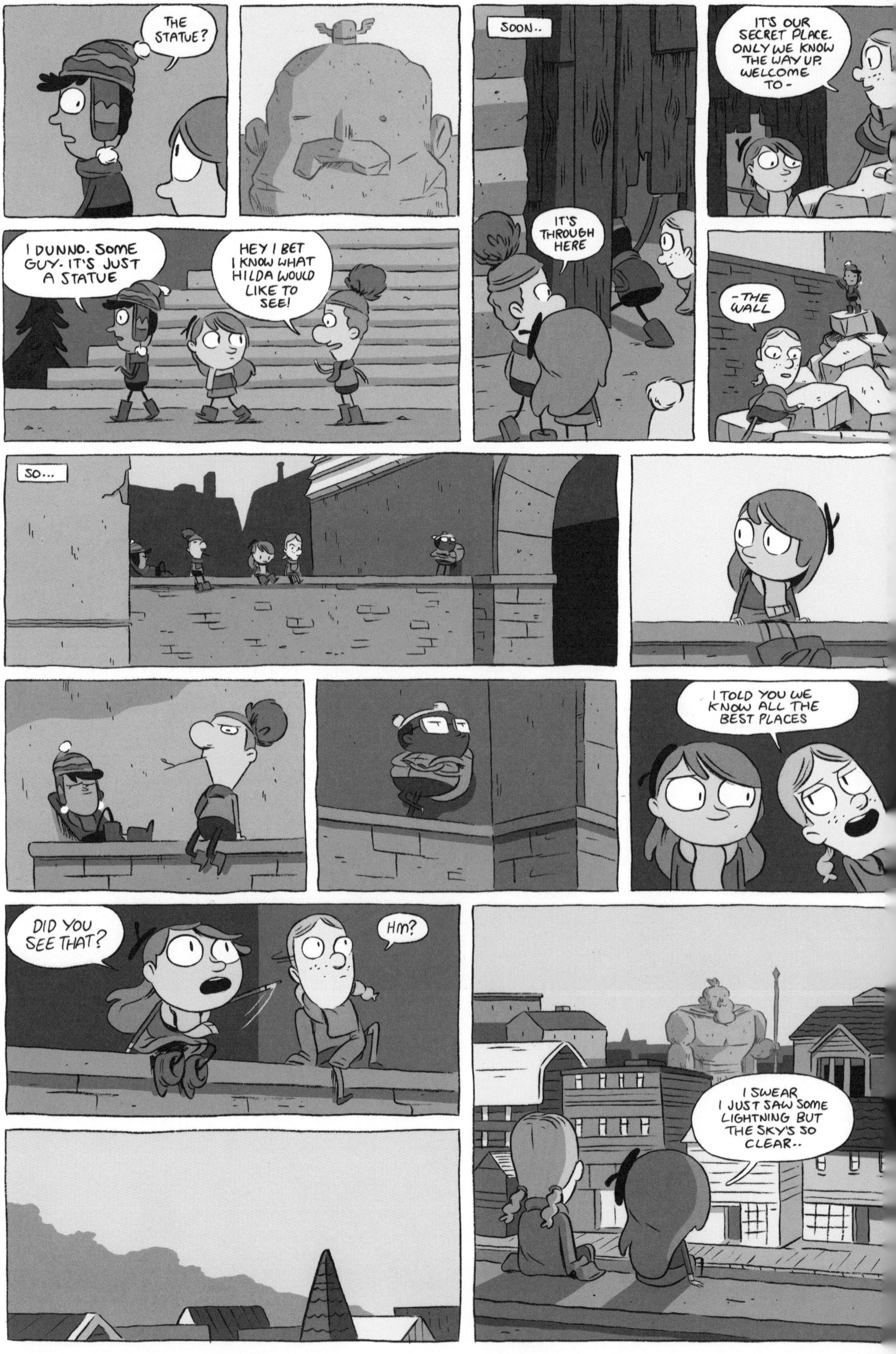
THE STATUE?
SOON..
IT'S THROUGH HERE
IT'S OUR SECRET PLACE. ONLY WE KNOW THE WAY UP. WELCOME TO -
I DUNNO. SOME GUY. IT'S JUST A STATUE
HEY I BET I KNOW WHAT HILDA WOULD LIKE TO SEE!
-THE WALL
SO...
I TOLD YOU WE KNOW ALL THE BEST PLACES
DID YOU SEE THAT?
Hm?
I SWEAR I JUST SAW SOME LIGHTNING BUT THE SKY'S SO CLEAR..

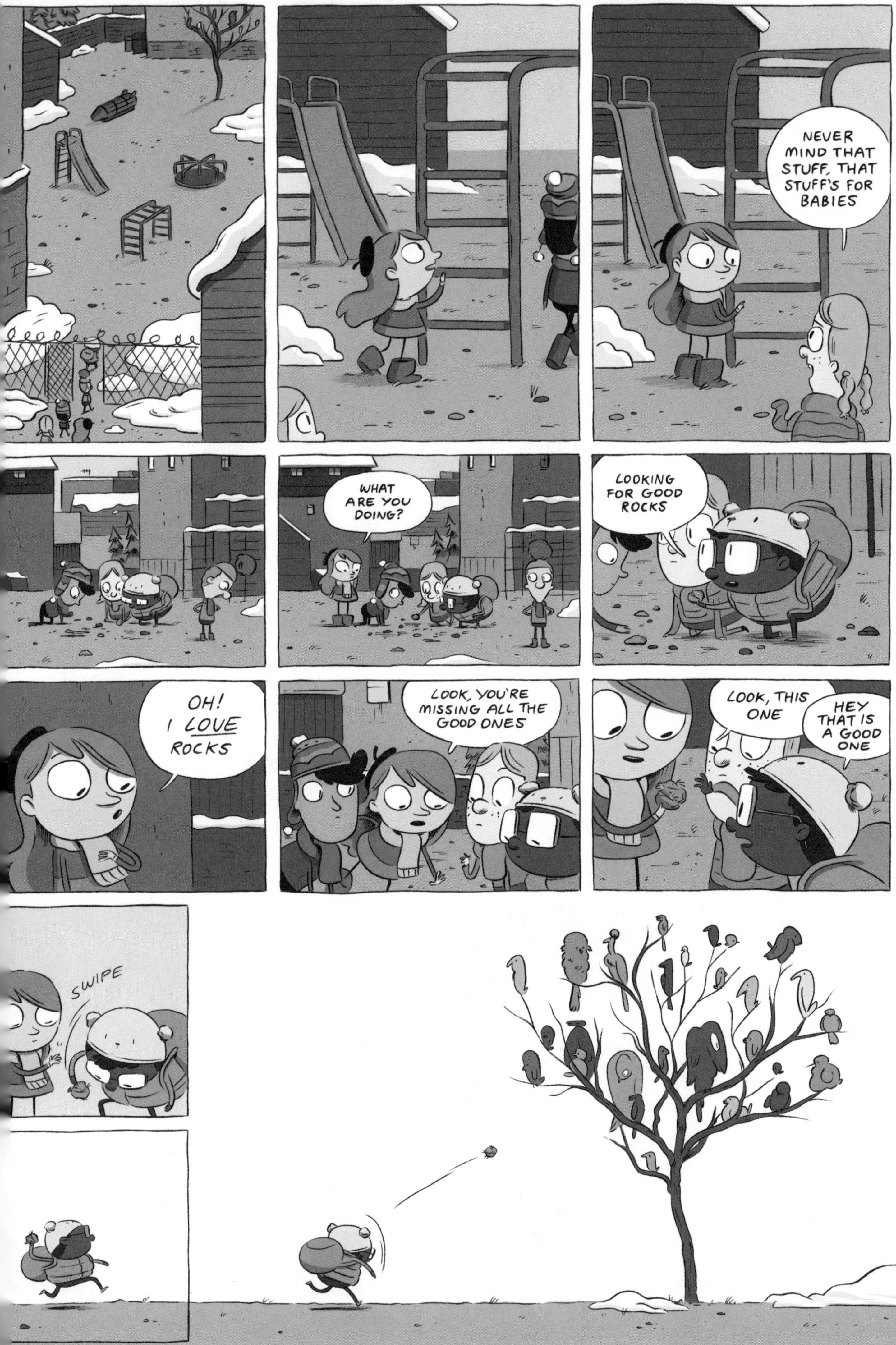
NEVER MIND THAT STUFF, THAT STUFF'S FOR BABIES
WHAT ARE YOU DOING?
LOOKING FOR GOOD ROCKS
OH! I LOVE ROCKS
LOOK, YOU'RE MISSING ALL THE GOOD ONES
LOOK, THIS ONE
HEY THAT IS A GOOD ONE
SWIPE

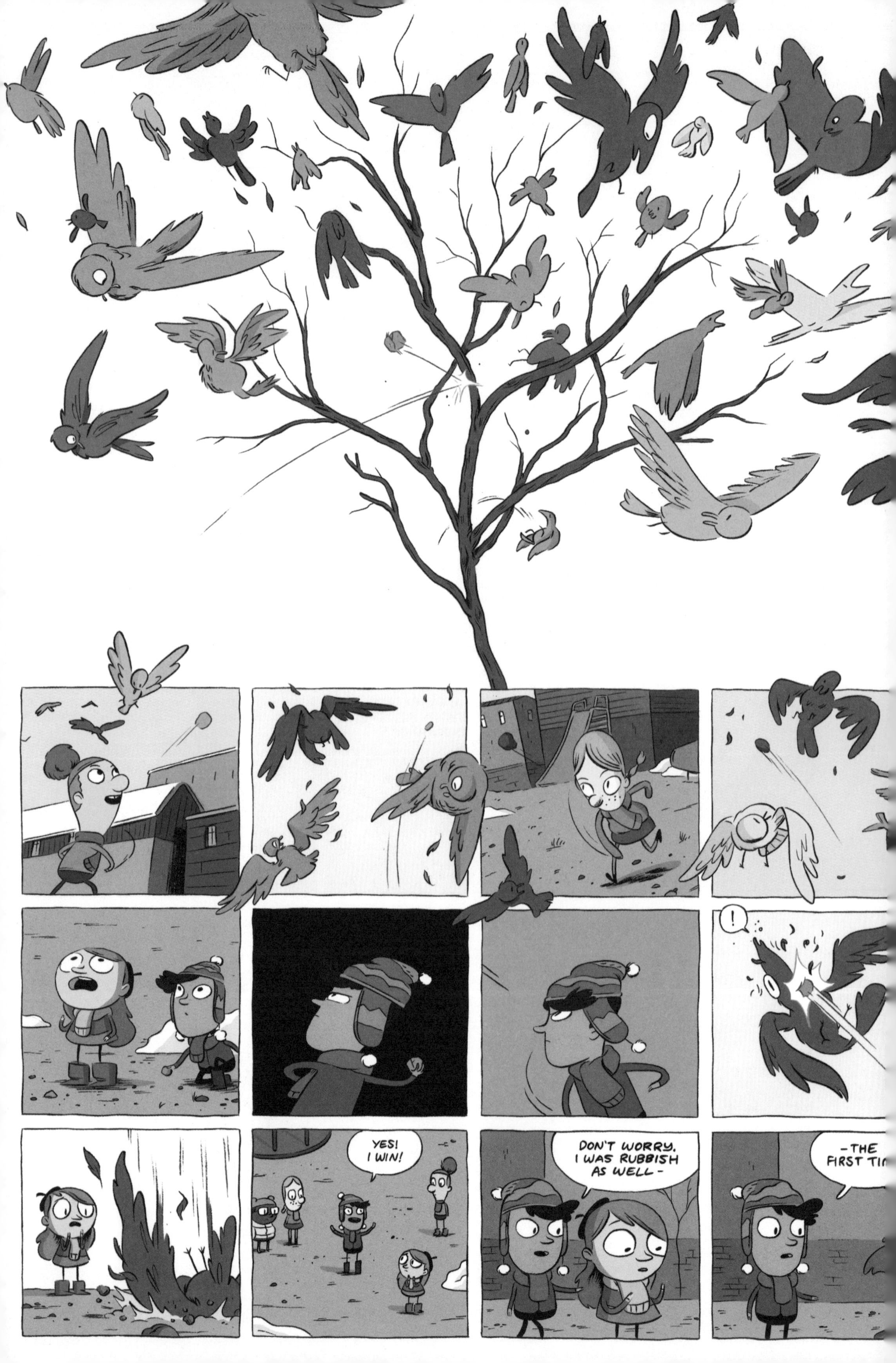

YES!
I WIN!
DON'T WORRY. I WAS RUBBISH AS WELL -
- THE FIRST TI

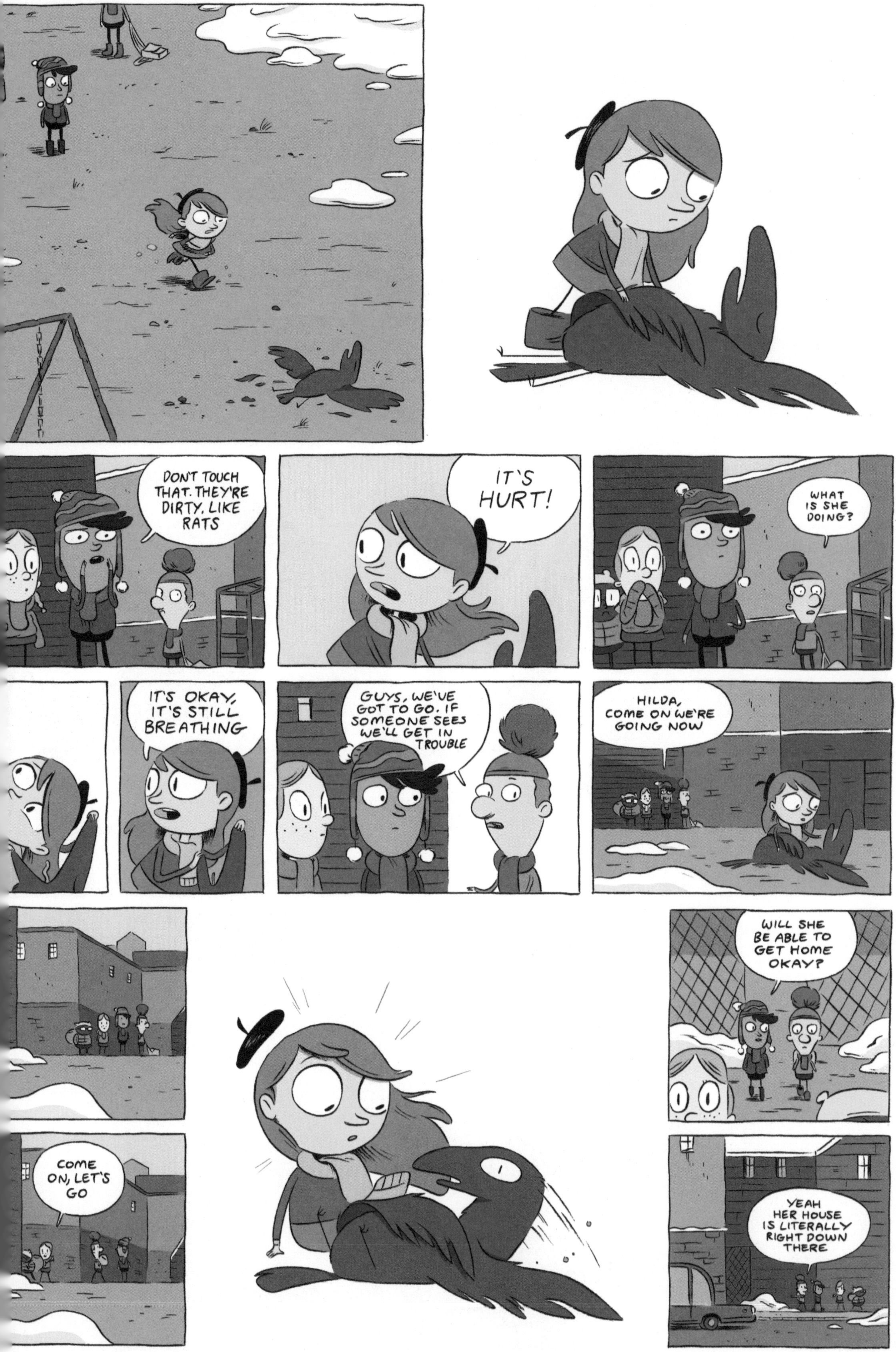

DON'T TOUCH THAT. THEY'RE DIRTY, LIKE RATS
IT'S HURT!
WHAT IS SHE DOING?
IT'S OKAY, IT'S STILL BREATHING
GUYS, WE'VE GOT TO GO. IF SOMEONE SEES WE'LL GET IN TROUBLE
HILDA, COME ON WE'RE GOING NOW
WILL SHE BE ABLE TO GET HOME OKAY?
COME ON, LET'S GO
YEAH HER HOUSE IS LITERALLY RIGHT DOWN THERE

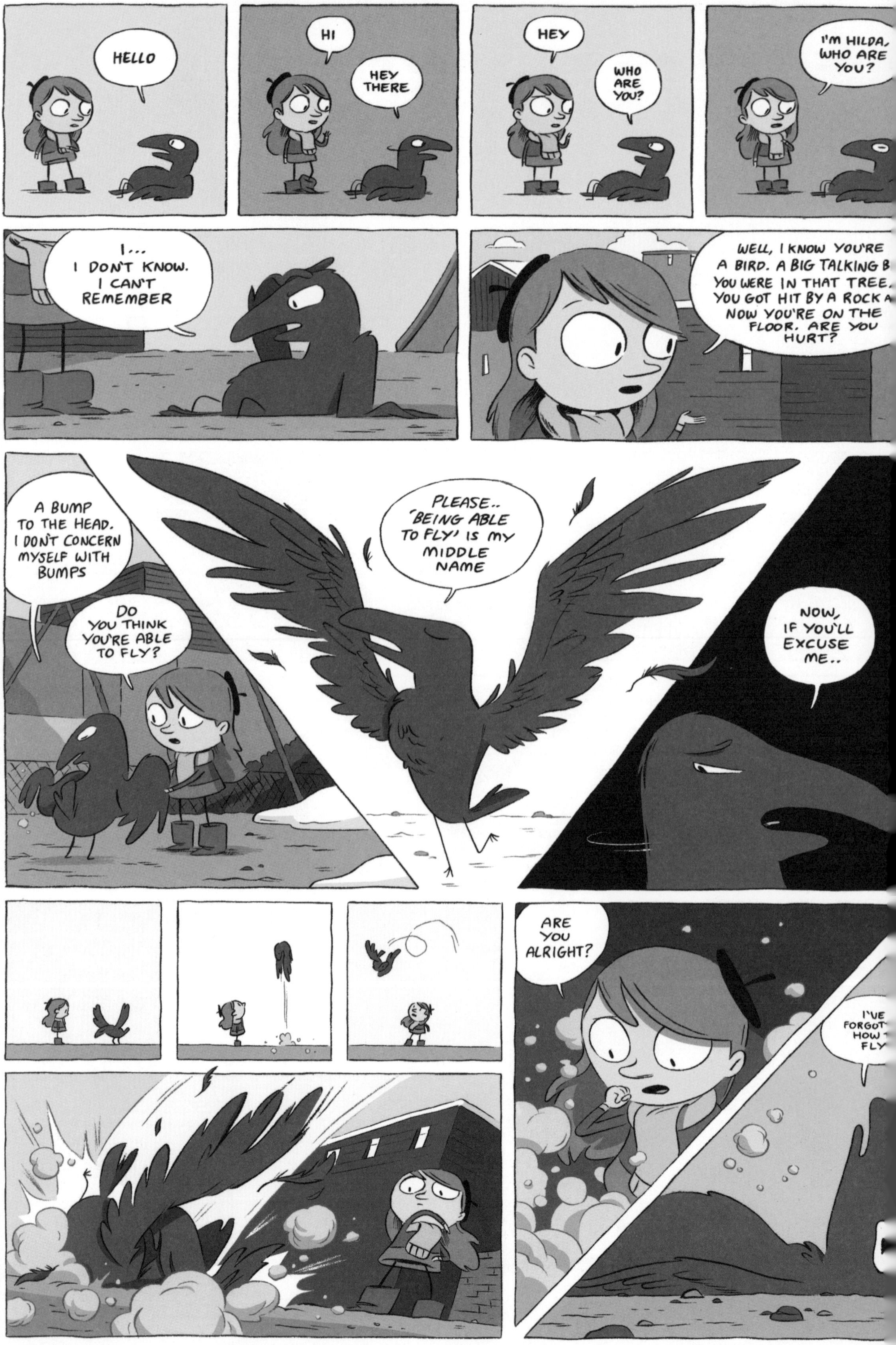
HELLO
HI
HEY THERE
HEY
WHO ARE YOU?
I'M HILDA, WHO ARE YOU?
I... I DON'T KNOW. I CAN'T REMEMBER
WELL, I KNOW YOU'RE A BIRD. A BIG TALKING
YOU WERE IN THAT TREE.
YOU GOT HIT BY A ROCK
NOW YOU'RE ON THE FLOOR. ARE YOU HURT?
A BUMP TO THE HEAD. I DON'T CONCERN MYSELF WITH BUMPS
DO YOU THINK YOU'RE ABLE TO FLY?
PLEASE.. 'BEING ABLE TO FLY' IS MY MIDDLE NAME
NOW, IF YOU'LL EXCUSE ME..
ARE YOU ALRIGHT?
I'VE

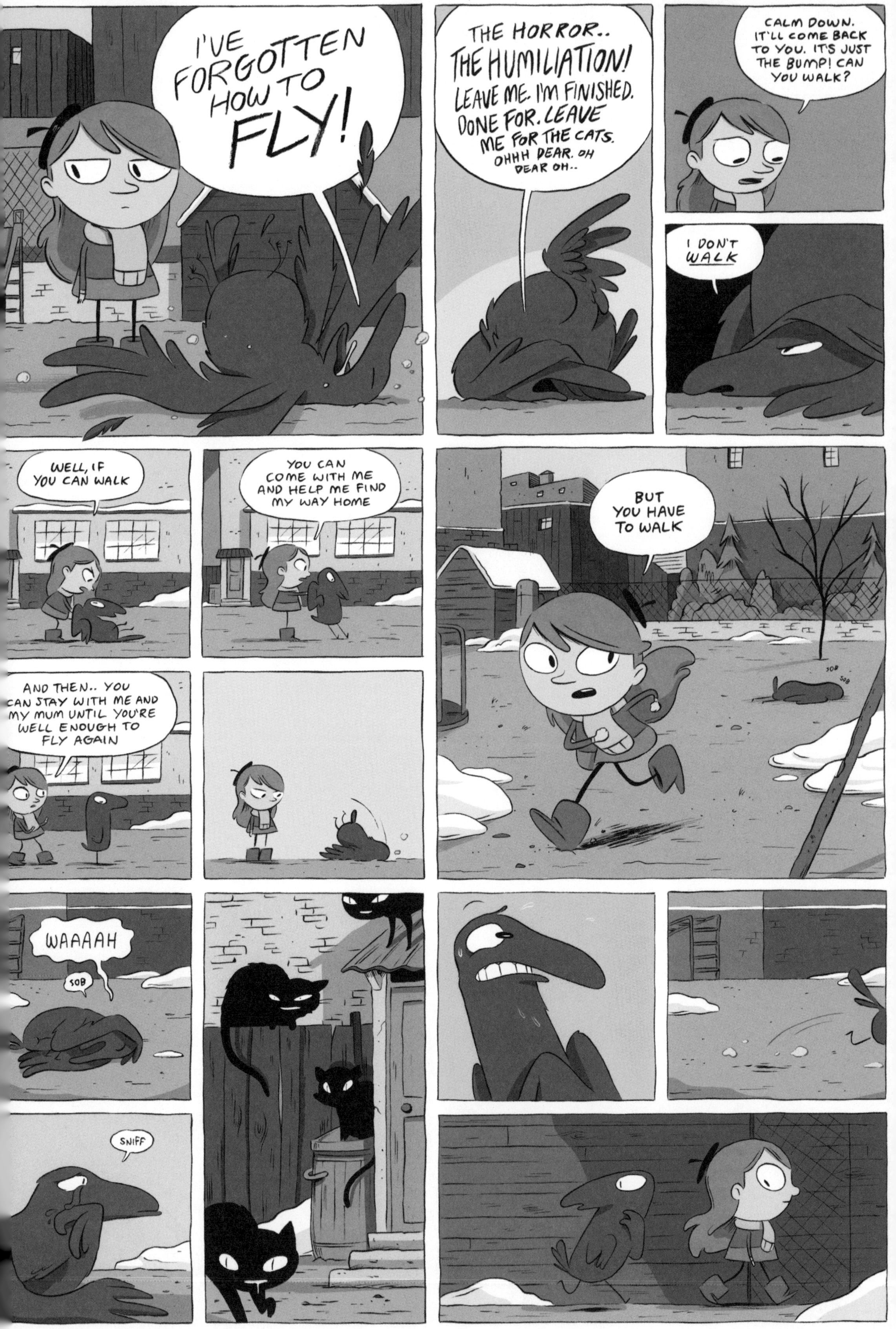
I'VE FORGOTTEN HOW TO FLY!
THE HORROR.. THE HUMILIATION! LEAVE ME. I'M FINISHED. DONE FOR. LEAVE ME FOR THE CATS. OHHH DEAR. OH DEAR OH..
CALM DOWN. IT'LL COME BACK TO YOU. IT'S JUST THE BUMP! CAN YOU WALK?
I DON'T WALK
WELL, IF YOU CAN WALK
YOU CAN COME WITH ME AND HELP ME FIND MY WAY HOME
BUT YOU HAVE TO WALK
AND THEN.. YOU CAN STAY WITH ME AND MY MUM UNTIL YOU'RE WELL ENOUGH TO FLY AGAIN
SOB
SOB
WAAAAH
SOB
SNIFF

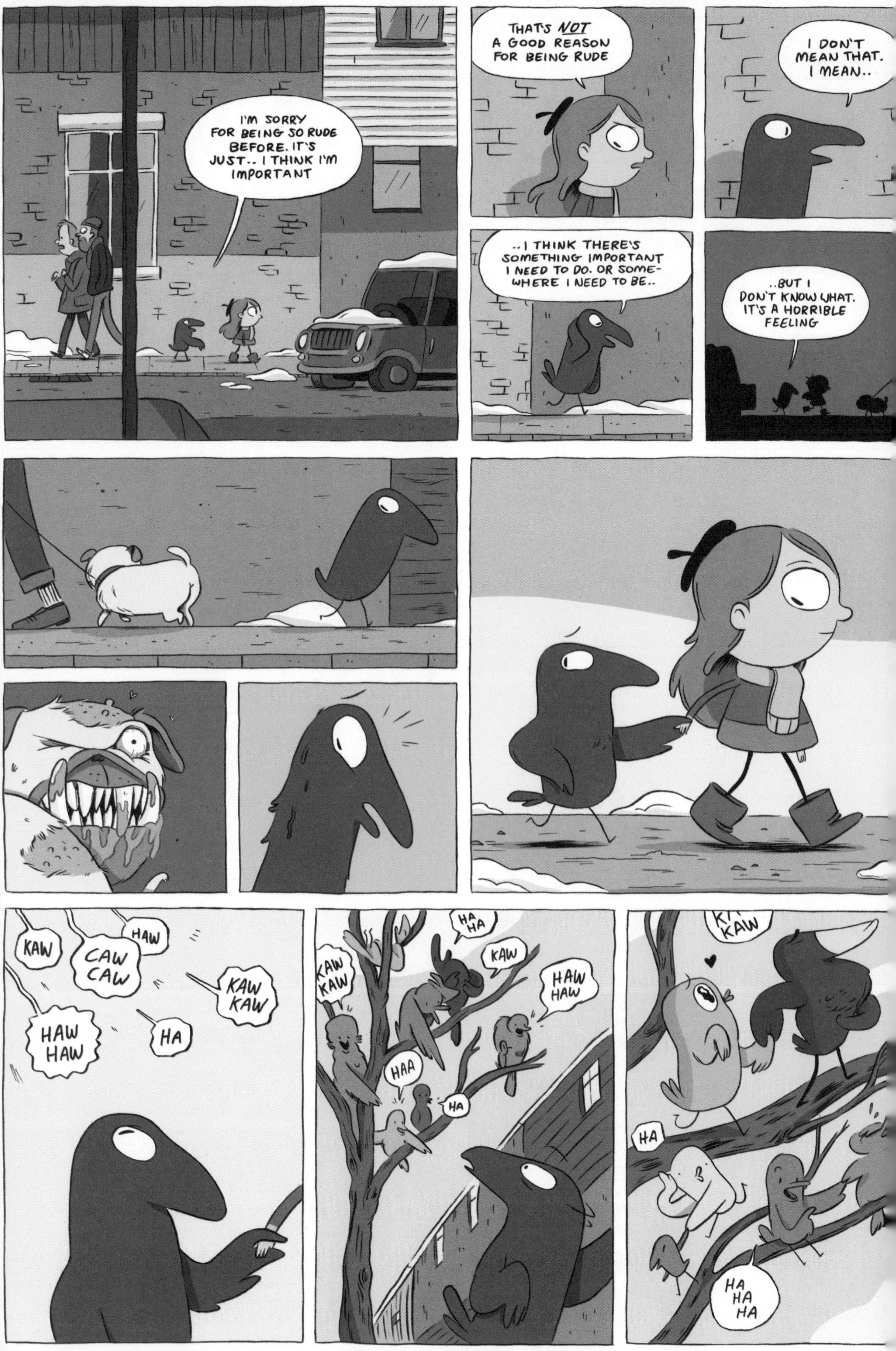

I'M SORRY FOR BEING SO RUDE BEFORE. IT'S JUST.. I THINK I'M IMPORTANT
THAT'S NOT A GOOD REASON FOR BEING RUDE
I DON'T MEAN THAT. I MEAN..
..I THINK THERE'S SOMETHING IMPORTANT I NEED TO DO. OR SOME-WHERE I NEED TO BE..
..BUT I DON'T KNOW WHAT. IT'S A HORRIBLE FEELING
KAW
CAW CAW
HAW
KAW KAW
HAW HAW
HA
KAW KAW
HA HA
KAW
HAW HAW
HAA
HA
KAW
HA
HA HA HA

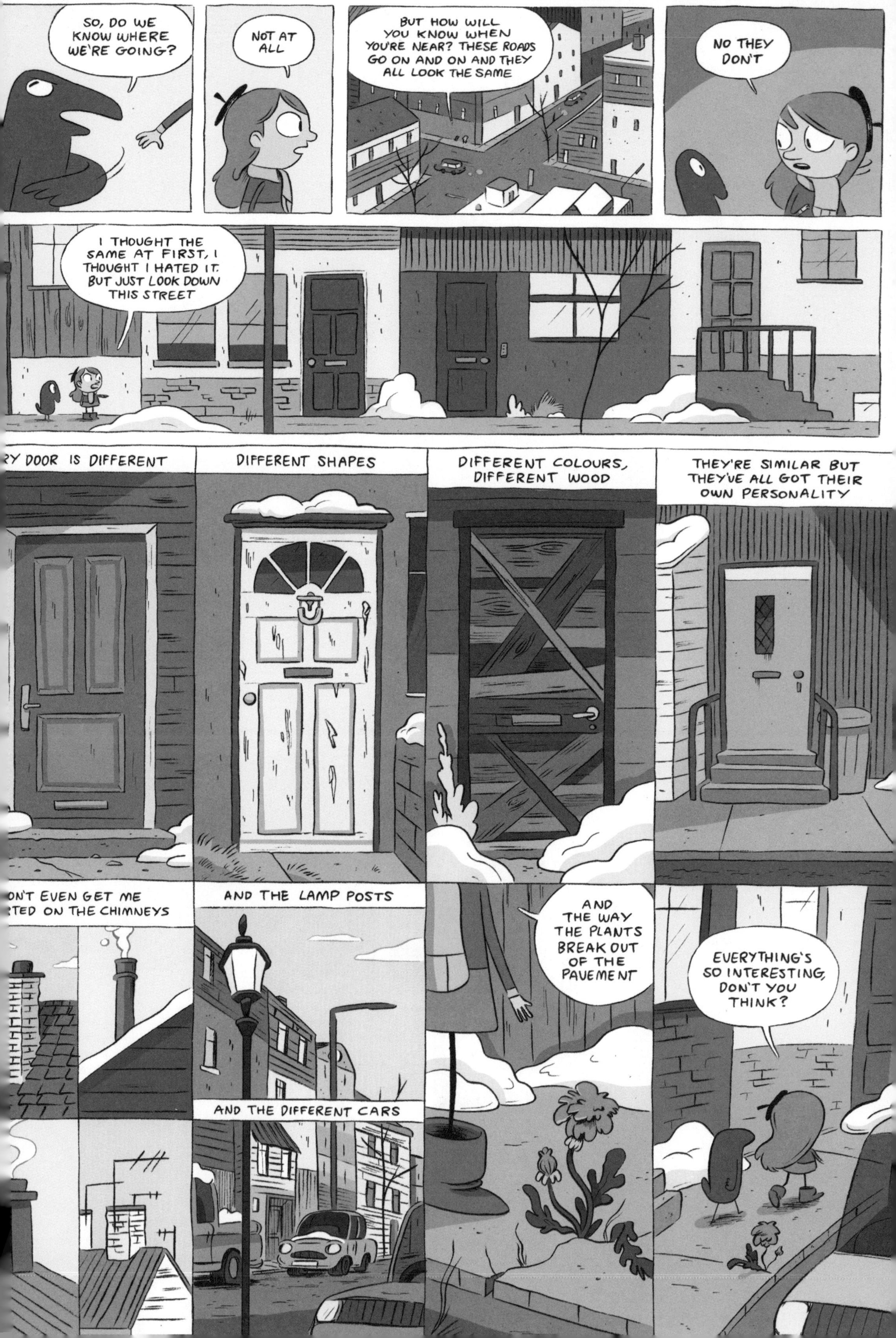
SO, DO WE KNOW WHERE WE'RE GOING?
NOT AT ALL
BUT HOW WILL YOU KNOW WHEN YOU'RE NEAR? THESE ROADS GO ON AND ON AND THEY ALL LOOK THE SAME
NO THEY DON'T
I THOUGHT THE SAME AT FIRST, I THOUGHT I HATED IT. BUT JUST LOOK DOWN THIS STREET
RY DOOR IS DIFFERENT
DIFFERENT SHAPES
DIFFERENT COLOURS, DIFFERENT WOOD
THEY'RE SIMILAR BUT THEY'VE ALL GOT THEIR OWN PERSONALITY
ON'T EVEN GET ME
RTED ON THE CHIMNEYS
AND THE LAMP POSTS
AND THE DIFFERENT CARS
AND THE WAY THE PLANTS BREAK OUT OF THE PAVEMENT
EVERYTHING'S SO INTERESTING, DON'T YOU THINK?

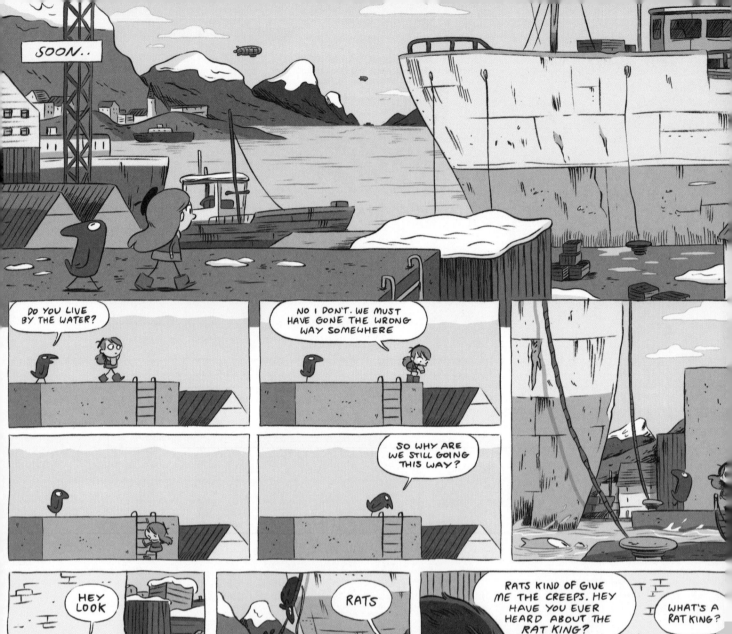

SOON..

DO YOU LIVE BY THE WATER?

NO I DON'T. WE MUST HAVE GONE THE WRONG WAY SOMEWHERE

SO WHY ARE WE STILL GOING THIS WAY?

HEY LOOK

RATS

RATS KIND OF GIVE ME THE CREEPS. HEY HAVE YOU EVER HEARD ABOUT THE RAT KING?

WHAT'S A RAT KING?

IT'S WHEN A BUNCH OF RATS GET THEIR TAILS ALL KNOTTED TOGETHER

THEY HAVE TO MOVE ABOUT AS ONE BIG HORRIBLE BALL..

..AND EVENTUALLY THEY MERGE TOGETHER INTO AN ENORMOUS, SCARY, RAT MONSTER

YOU CAN'T REMEMBER WHO YOU ARE BUT YOU CAN REMEMBER *THAT*?

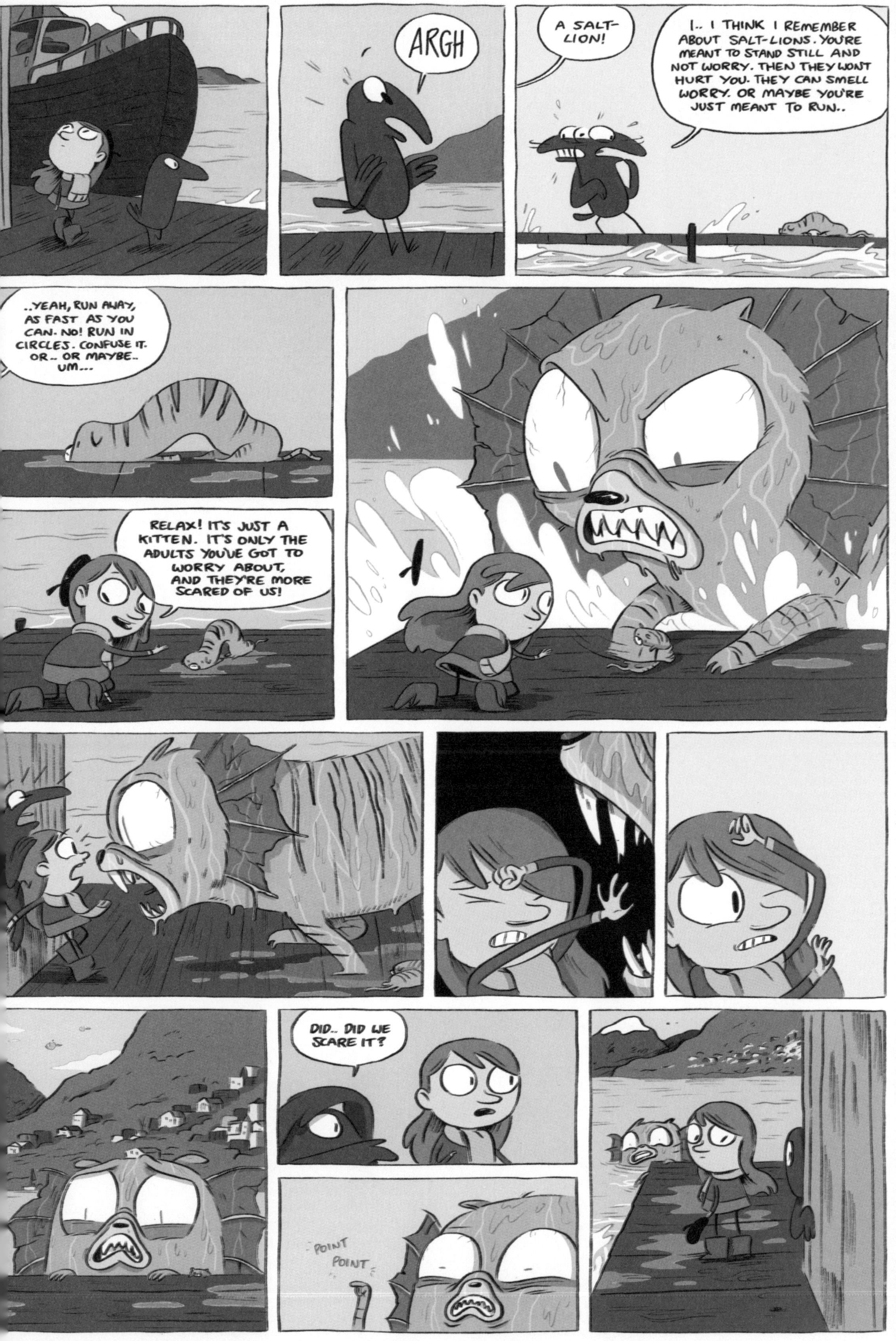
ARGH
A SALT-LION!
I.. I THINK I REMEMBER ABOUT SALT-LIONS. YOU'RE MEANT TO STAND STILL AND NOT WORRY. THEN THEY WON'T HURT YOU. THEY CAN SMELL WORRY. OR MAYBE YOU'RE JUST MEANT TO RUN..
..YEAH, RUN AWAY, AS FAST AS YOU CAN. NO! RUN IN CIRCLES. CONFUSE IT. OR.. OR MAYBE.. UM...
RELAX! IT'S JUST A KITTEN. IT'S ONLY THE ADULTS YOU'VE GOT TO WORRY ABOUT, AND THEY'RE MORE SCARED OF US!
DID.. DID WE SCARE IT?
POINT POINT

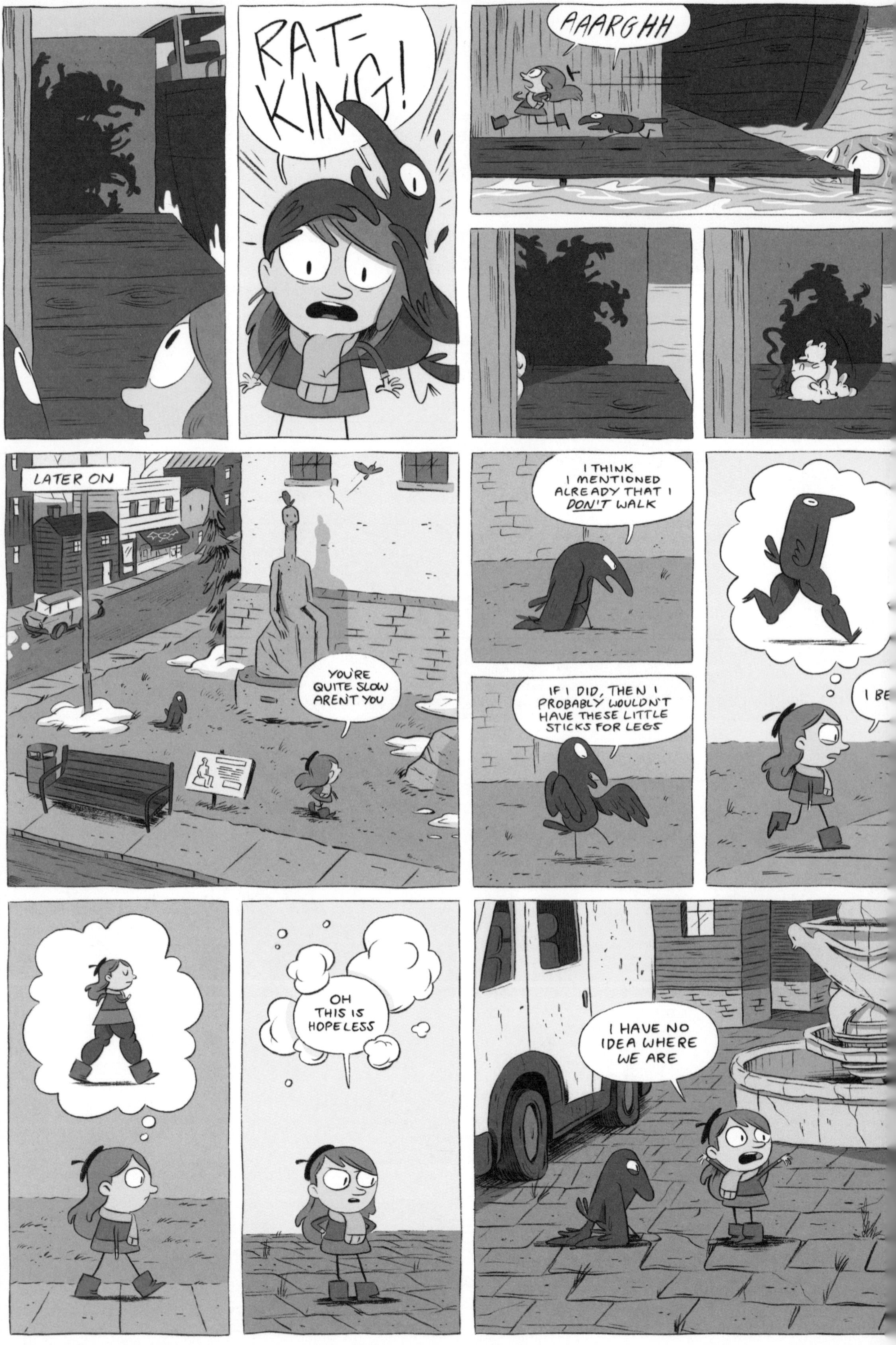
RAT-KING!
AAARGHH
LATER ON
YOU'RE QUITE SLOW AREN'T YOU
I THINK I MENTIONED ALREADY THAT I DON'T WALK
IF I DID, THEN I PROBABLY WOULDN'T HAVE THESE LITTLE STICKS FOR LEGS
I BE
OH THIS IS HOPELESS
I HAVE NO IDEA WHERE WE ARE

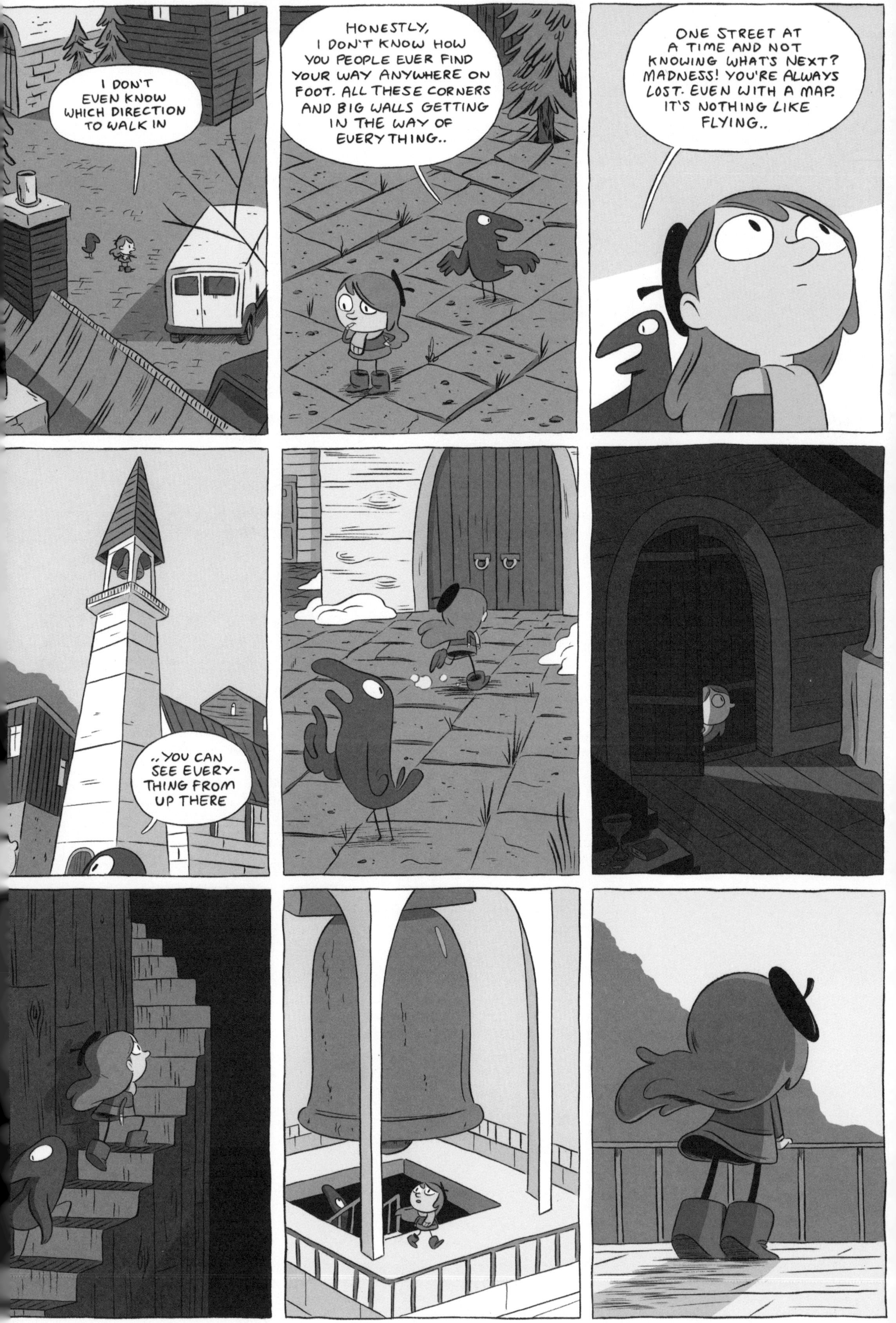
I DON'T EVEN KNOW WHICH DIRECTION TO WALK IN
HONESTLY, I DON'T KNOW HOW YOU PEOPLE EVER FIND YOUR WAY ANYWHERE ON FOOT. ALL THESE CORNERS AND BIG WALLS GETTING IN THE WAY OF EVERYTHING..
ONE STREET AT A TIME AND NOT KNOWING WHAT'S NEXT? MADNESS! YOU'RE ALWAYS LOST. EVEN WITH A MAP. IT'S NOTHING LIKE FLYING..
..YOU CAN SEE EVERY-THING FROM UP THERE

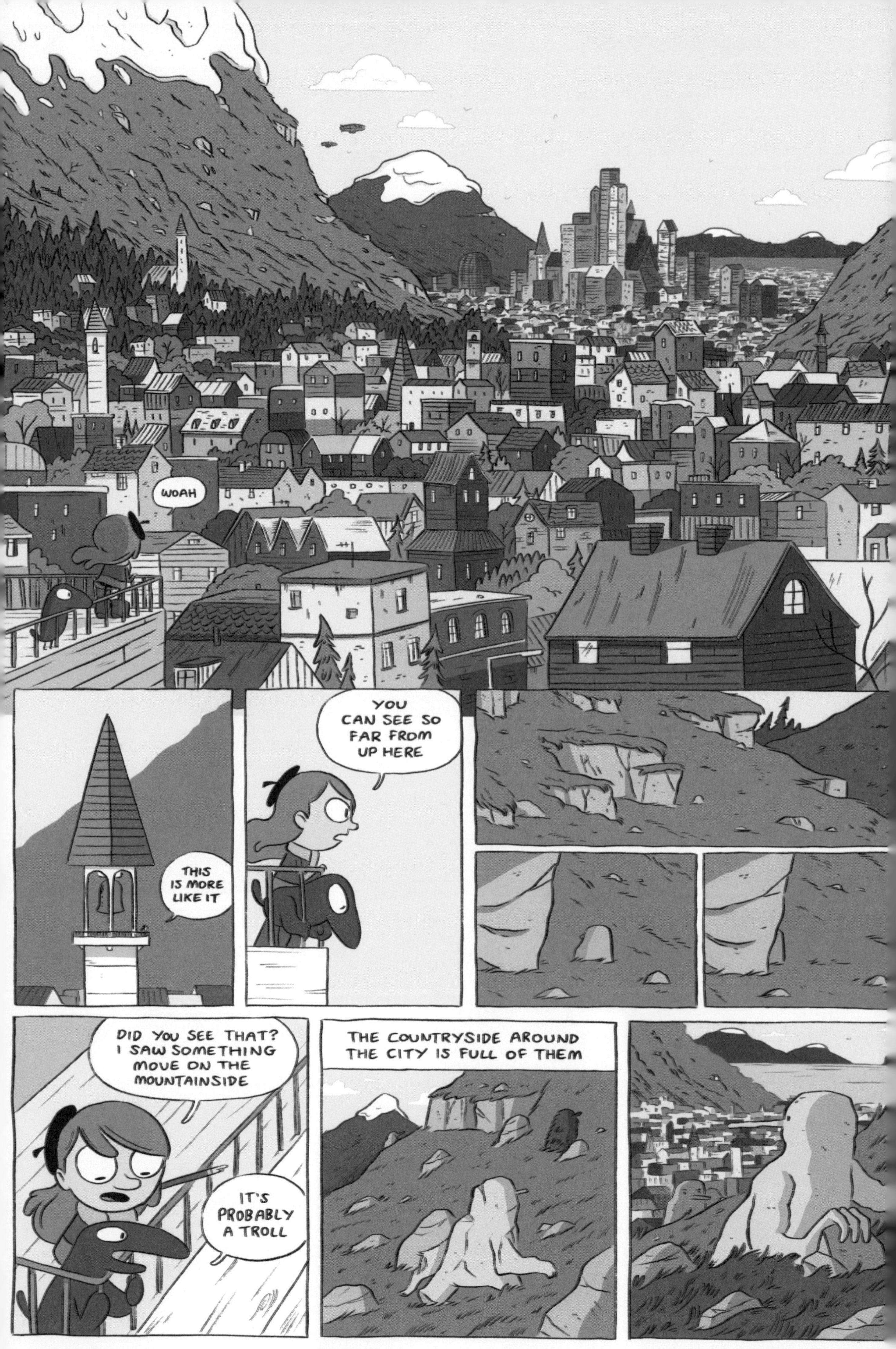
WOAH
THIS IS MORE LIKE IT
YOU CAN SEE SO FAR FROM UP HERE
DID YOU SEE THAT? I SAW SOMETHING MOVE ON THE MOUNTAINSIDE
IT'S PROBABLY A TROLL
THE COUNTRYSIDE AROUND THE CITY IS FULL OF THEM

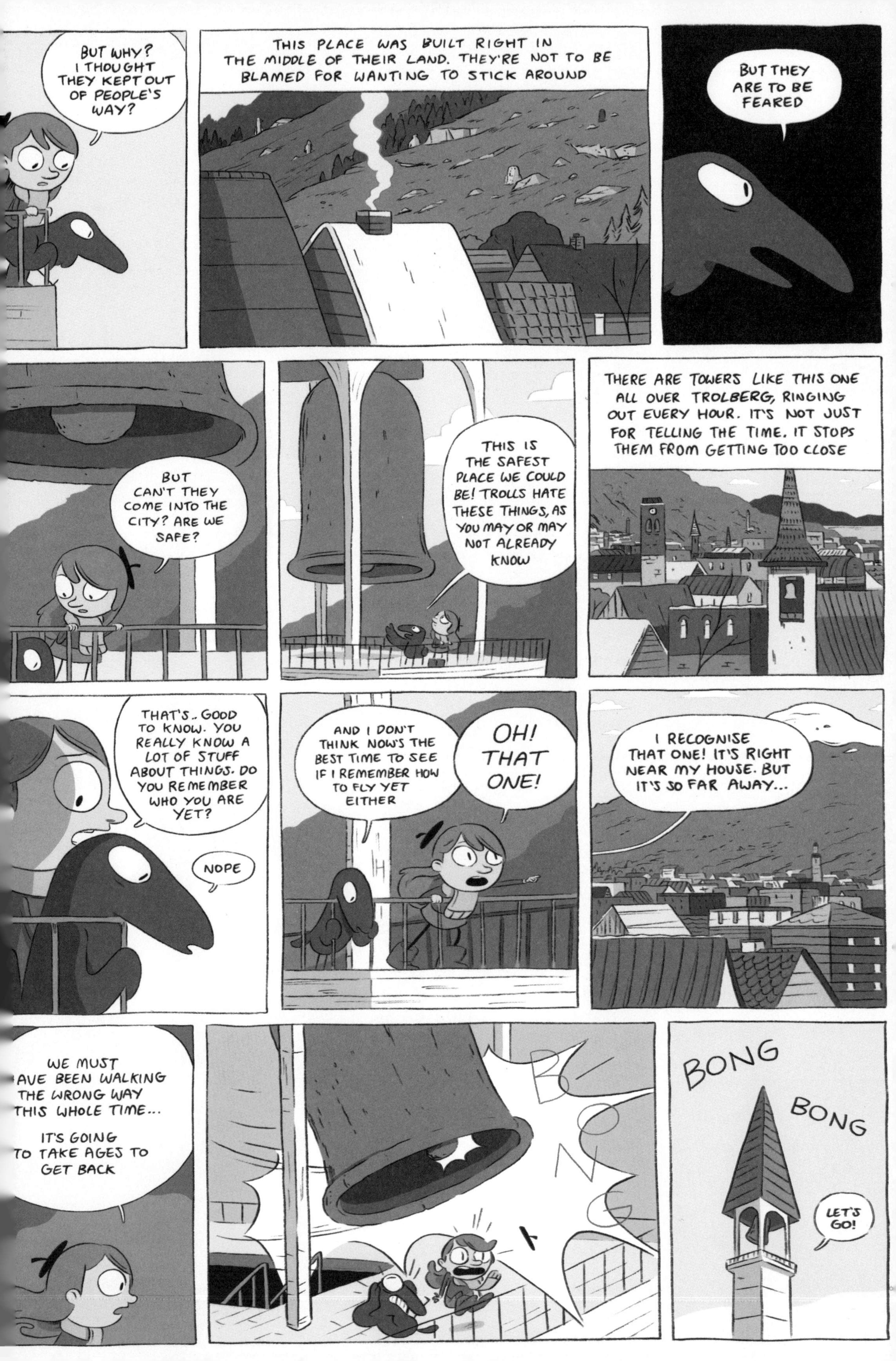
BUT WHY? I THOUGHT THEY KEPT OUT OF PEOPLE'S WAY?
THIS PLACE WAS BUILT RIGHT IN THE MIDDLE OF THEIR LAND. THEY'RE NOT TO BE BLAMED FOR WANTING TO STICK AROUND
BUT THEY ARE TO BE FEARED
BUT CAN'T THEY COME INTO THE CITY? ARE WE SAFE?
THIS IS THE SAFEST PLACE WE COULD BE! TROLLS HATE THESE THINGS, AS YOU MAY OR MAY NOT ALREADY KNOW
THERE ARE TOWERS LIKE THIS ONE ALL OVER TROLBERG, RINGING OUT EVERY HOUR. IT'S NOT JUST FOR TELLING THE TIME. IT STOPS THEM FROM GETTING TOO CLOSE
THAT'S.. GOOD TO KNOW. YOU REALLY KNOW A LOT OF STUFF ABOUT THINGS. DO YOU REMEMBER WHO YOU ARE YET?
NOPE
AND I DON'T THINK NOW'S THE BEST TIME TO SEE IF I REMEMBER HOW TO FLY YET EITHER
OH! THAT ONE!
I RECOGNISE THAT ONE! IT'S RIGHT NEAR MY HOUSE. BUT IT'S SO FAR AWAY...
WE MUST AVE BEEN WALKING THE WRONG WAY THIS WHOLE TIME...
IT'S GOING TO TAKE AGES TO GET BACK
BONG
BONG
BONG
LET'S GO!

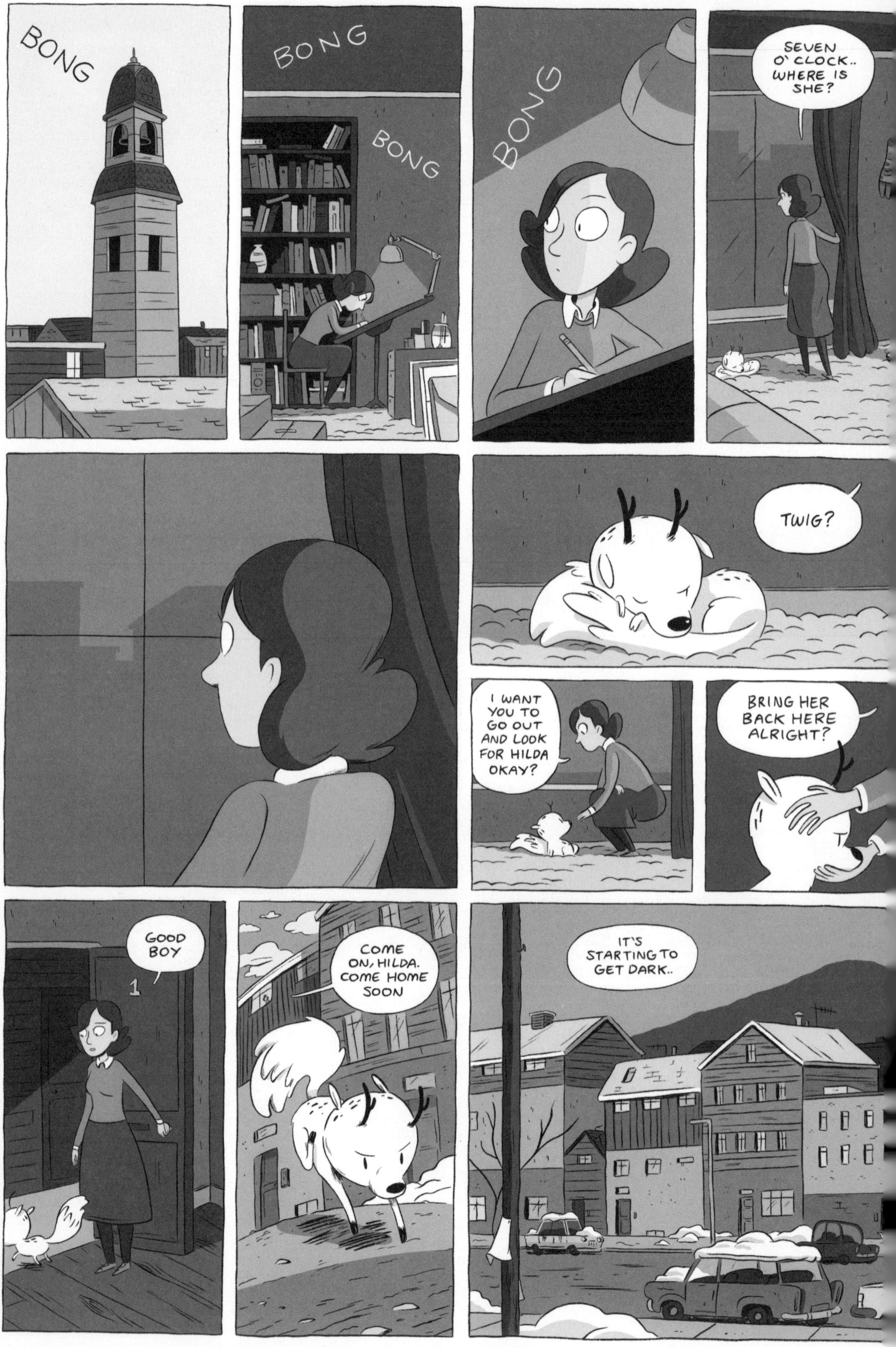
BONG
BONG
BONG
BONG
SEVEN O' CLOCK.. WHERE IS SHE?
TWIG?
I WANT YOU TO GO OUT AND LOOK FOR HILDA OKAY?
BRING HER BACK HERE ALRIGHT?
GOOD BOY
1
COME ON, HILDA. COME HOME SOON
IT'S STARTING TO GET DARK..

IT'S STARTING TO GET DARK!

YOU CAN TELL IT'S GETTING DARK BECAUSE PEOPLE ARE STARTING TO PUT THEIR LIGHTS ON

THEY LOOK SO COSY FROM OUT HERE

JT YOU JUST W THE PEOPLE IDE HAVE NO A HOW COSY THEY ARE

HEY LOOK, THEY'RE LIGHTING SOME LANTERNS DOWN THERE

THEY MUST BE FOR THE PARADE

IT MUST BE STARTING REALLY SOON... WHERE DID THE DAY GO?

ARADE..?

WE REALLY SHOULD HURRY UP. I THINK MUM MIGHT BE UPSET IF WE MISSED IT. SHE SEEMED REALLY KEEN ON GOING.

HMM..

COME ON

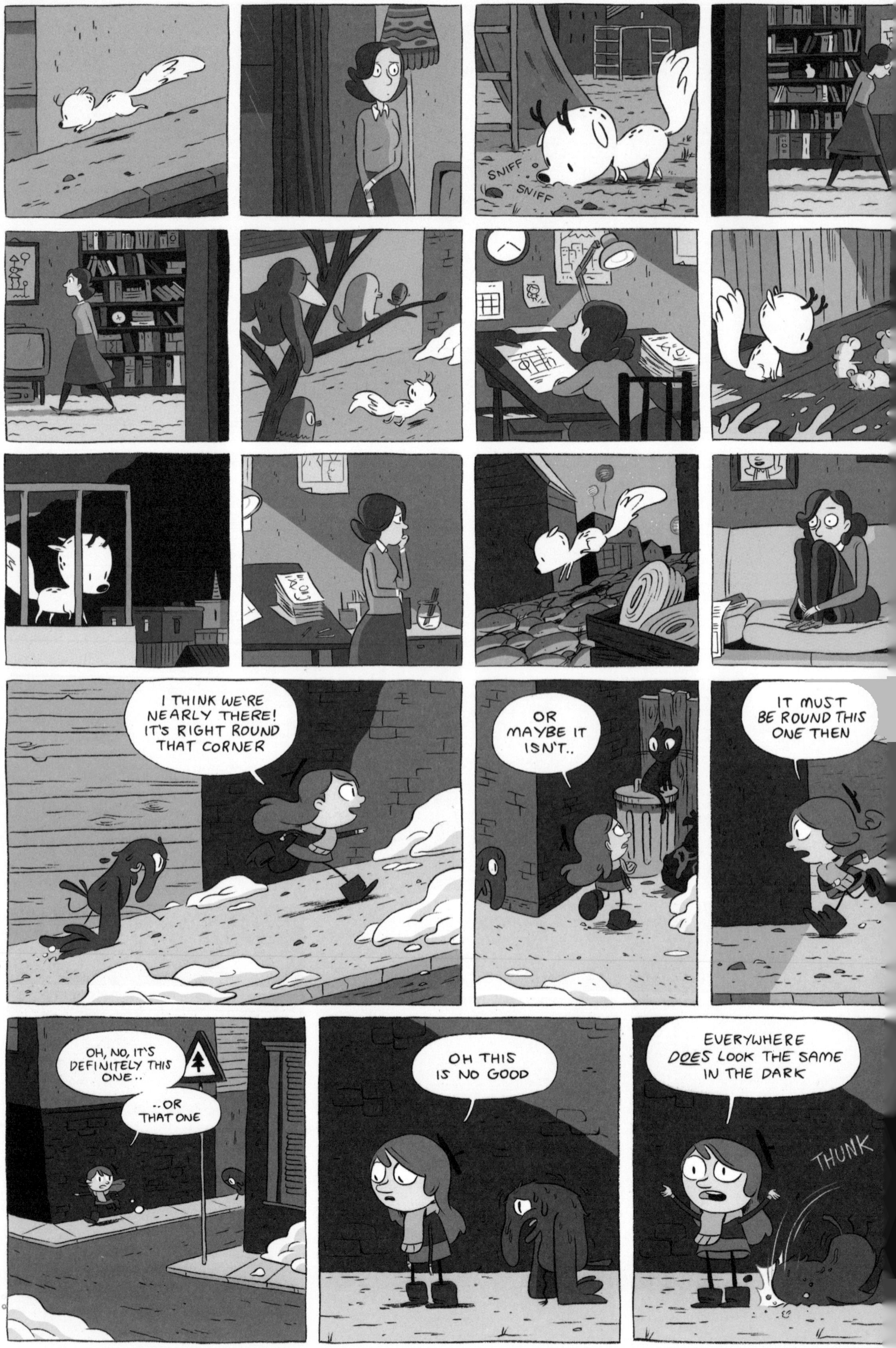
SNIFF
SNIFF
I THINK WE'RE NEARLY THERE! IT'S RIGHT ROUND THAT CORNER
OR MAYBE IT ISN'T..
IT MUST BE ROUND THIS ONE THEN
OH, NO, IT'S DEFINITELY THIS ONE..
..OR THAT ONE
OH THIS IS NO GOOD
EVERYWHERE DOES LOOK THE SAME IN THE DARK
THUNK

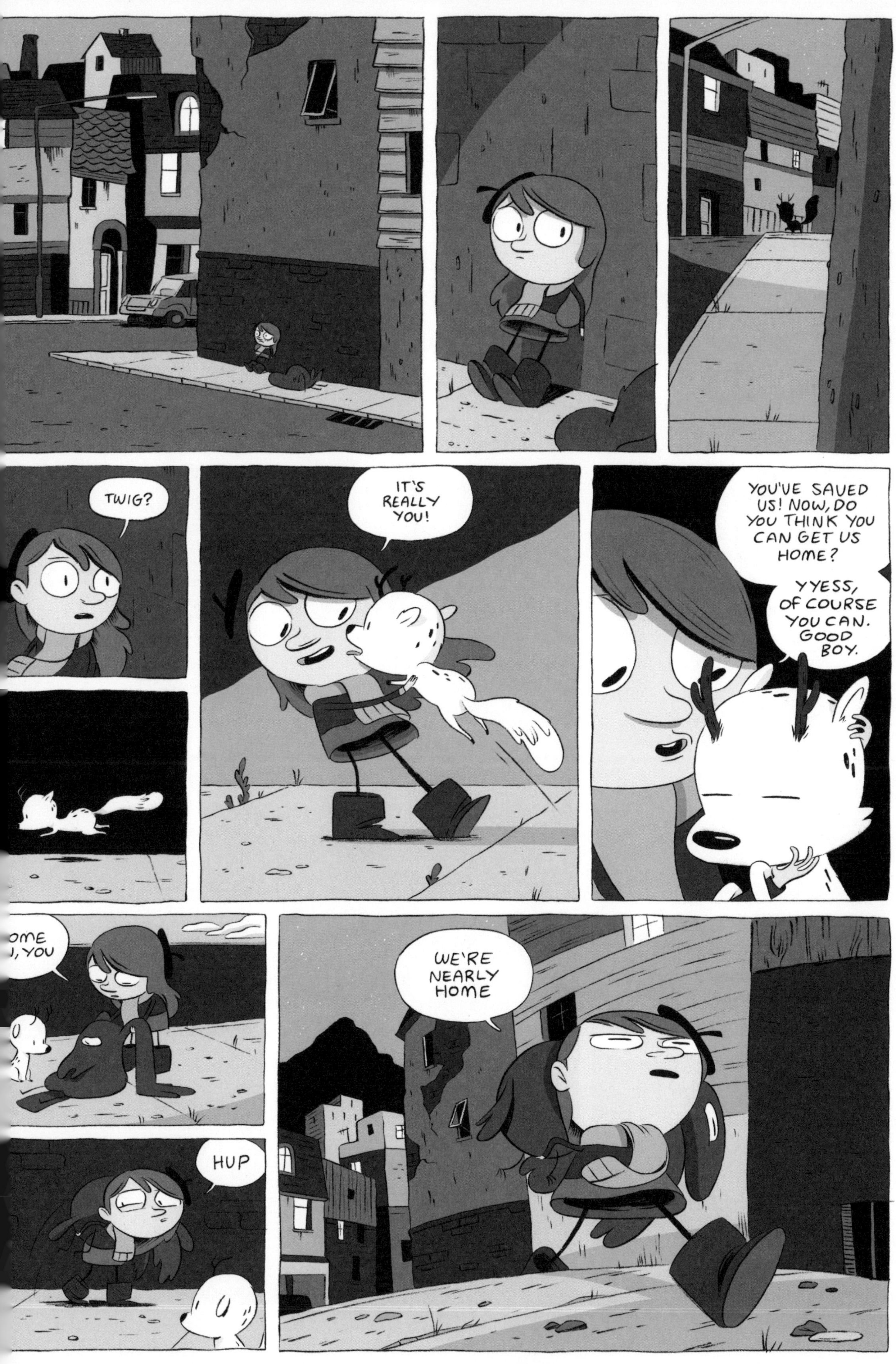
TWIG?
IT'S REALLY YOU!
YOU'VE SAVED US! NOW, DO YOU THINK YOU CAN GET US HOME?
YYESS, OF COURSE YOU CAN. GOOD BOY.
OME
, YOU
HUP
WE'RE NEARLY HOME

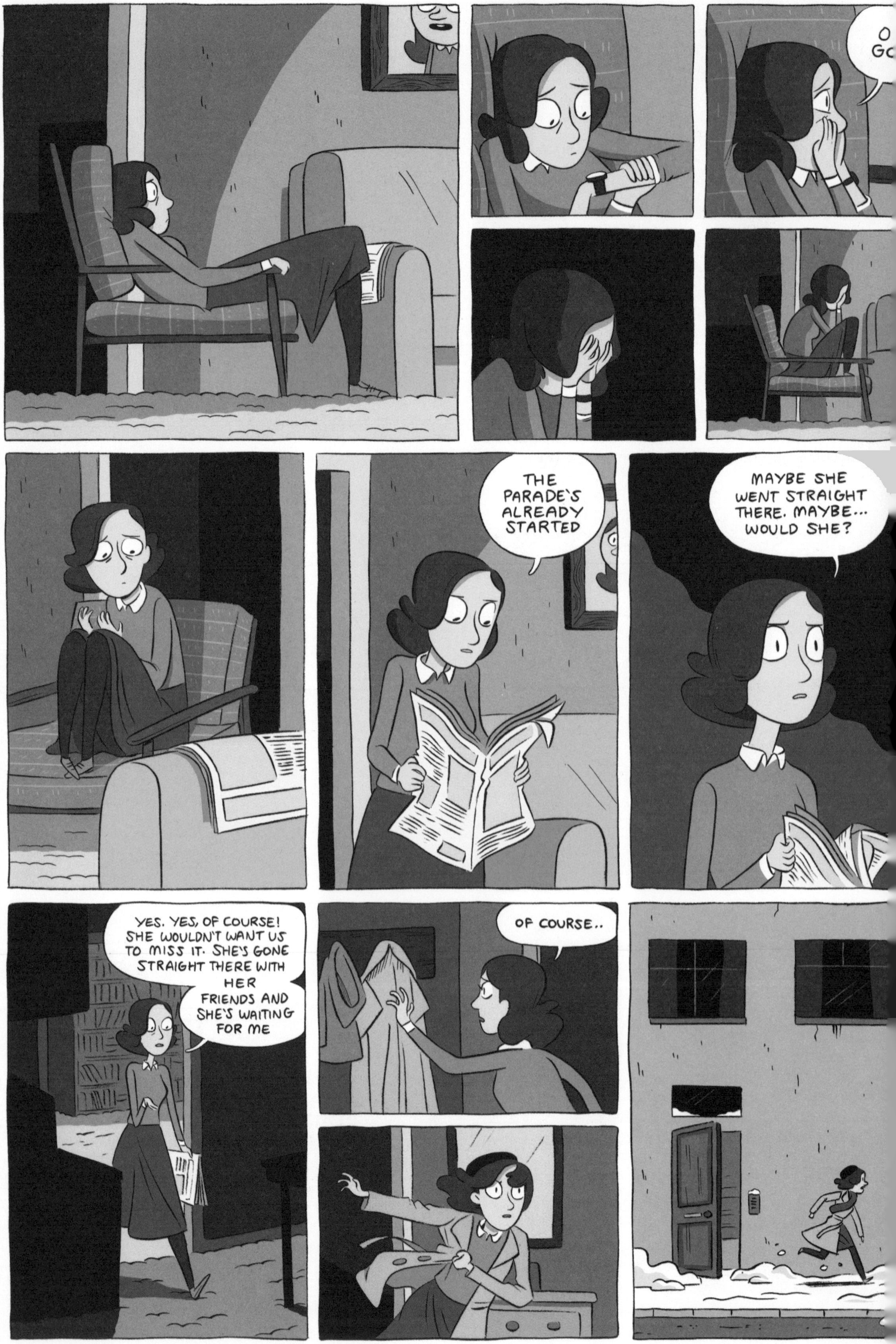
THE PARADE'S ALREADY STARTED
MAYBE SHE WENT STRAIGHT THERE. MAYBE... WOULD SHE?
YES. YES, OF COURSE! SHE WOULDN'T WANT US TO MISS IT. SHE'S GONE STRAIGHT THERE WITH HER FRIENDS AND SHE'S WAITING FOR ME
OF COURSE..

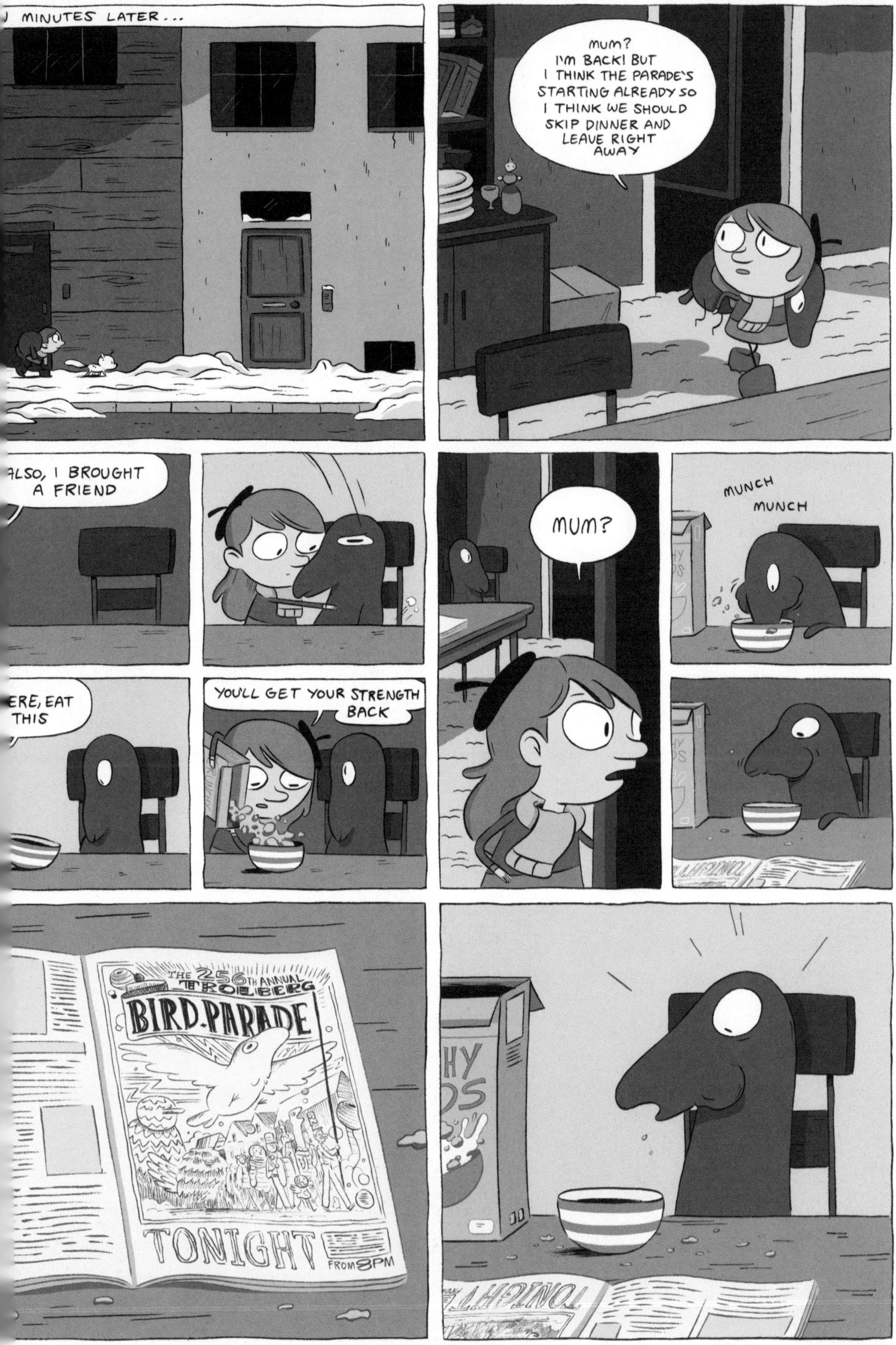
MINUTES LATER...
MUM? I'M BACK! BUT I THINK THE PARADE'S STARTING ALREADY SO I THINK WE SHOULD SKIP DINNER AND LEAVE RIGHT AWAY
ALSO, I BROUGHT A FRIEND
ERE, EAT THIS
YOU'LL GET YOUR STRENGTH BACK
MUM?
MUNCH
MUNCH
THE 256TH ANNUAL TROLBERG
BIRD PARADE
TONIGHT
FROM 8PM

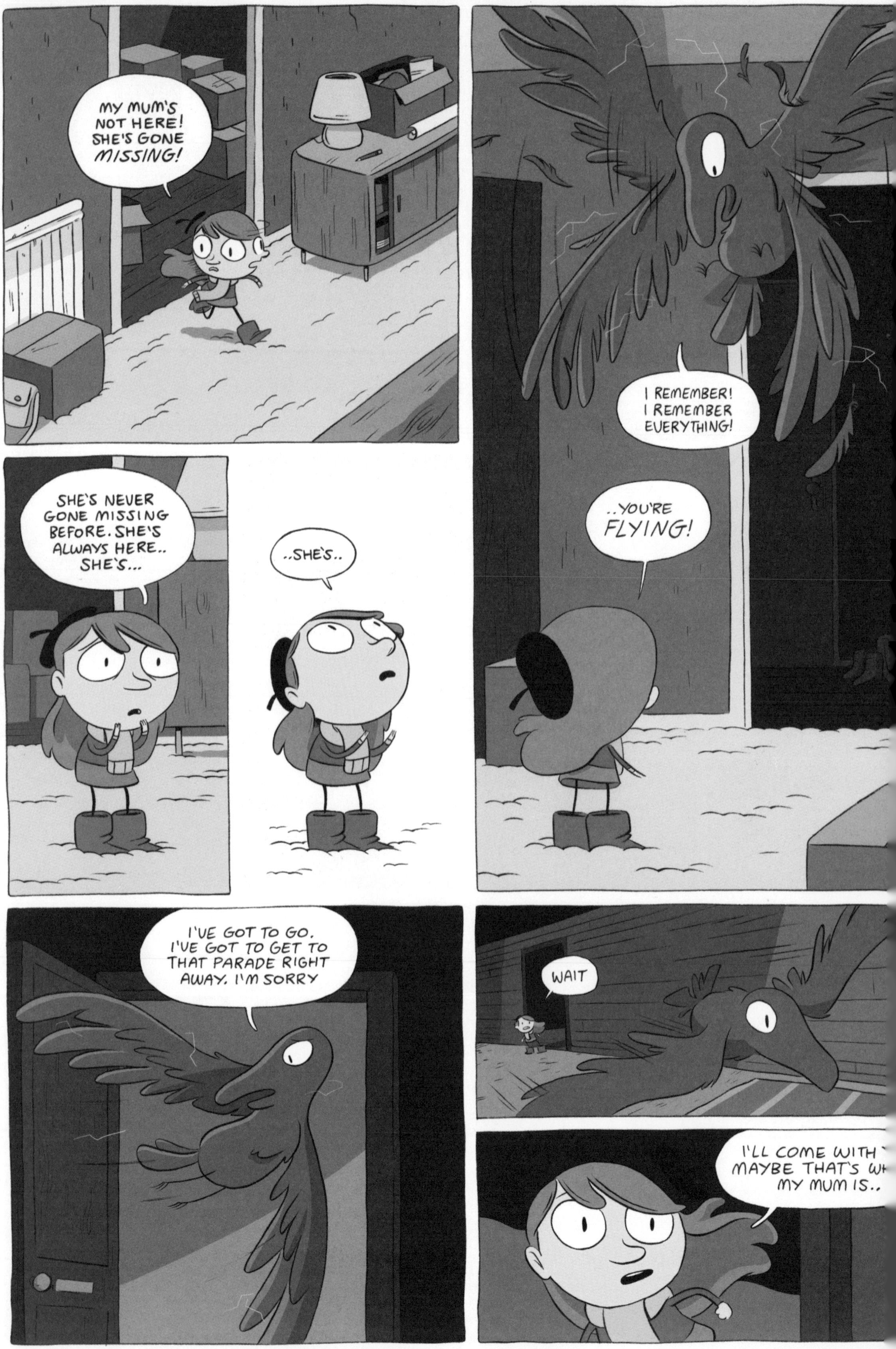
MY MUM'S NOT HERE! SHE'S GONE MISSING!
I REMEMBER! I REMEMBER EVERYTHING!
SHE'S NEVER GONE MISSING BEFORE. SHE'S ALWAYS HERE.. SHE'S...
..SHE'S..
..YOU'RE FLYING!
I'VE GOT TO GO. I'VE GOT TO GET TO THAT PARADE RIGHT AWAY. I'M SORRY
WAIT
I'LL COME WITH
MAYBE THAT'S WH
MY MUM IS..

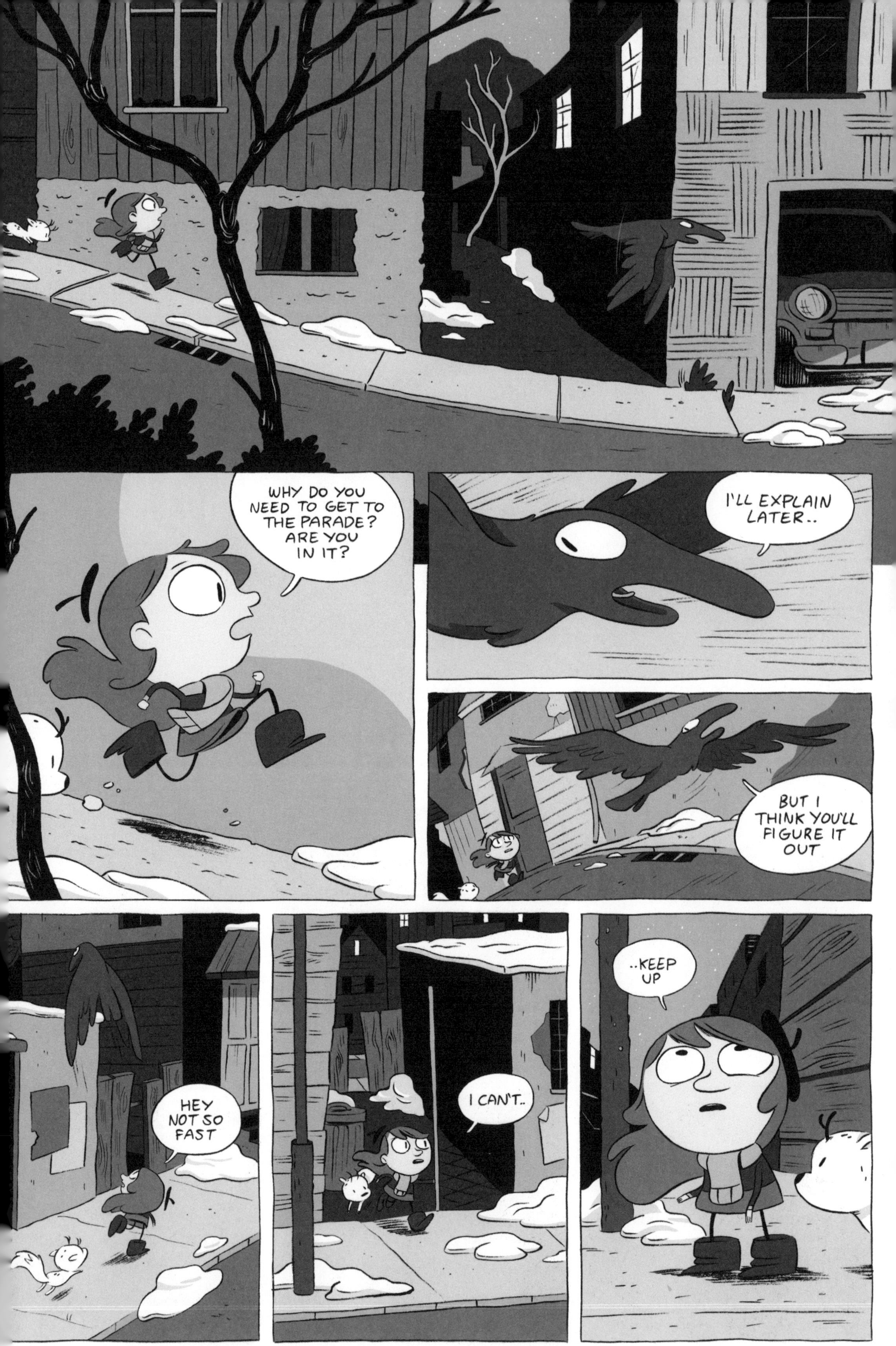
WHY DO YOU NEED TO GET TO THE PARADE? ARE YOU IN IT?
I'LL EXPLAIN LATER..
BUT I THINK YOU'LL FIGURE IT OUT
HEY NOT SO FAST
I CAN'T..
..KEEP UP

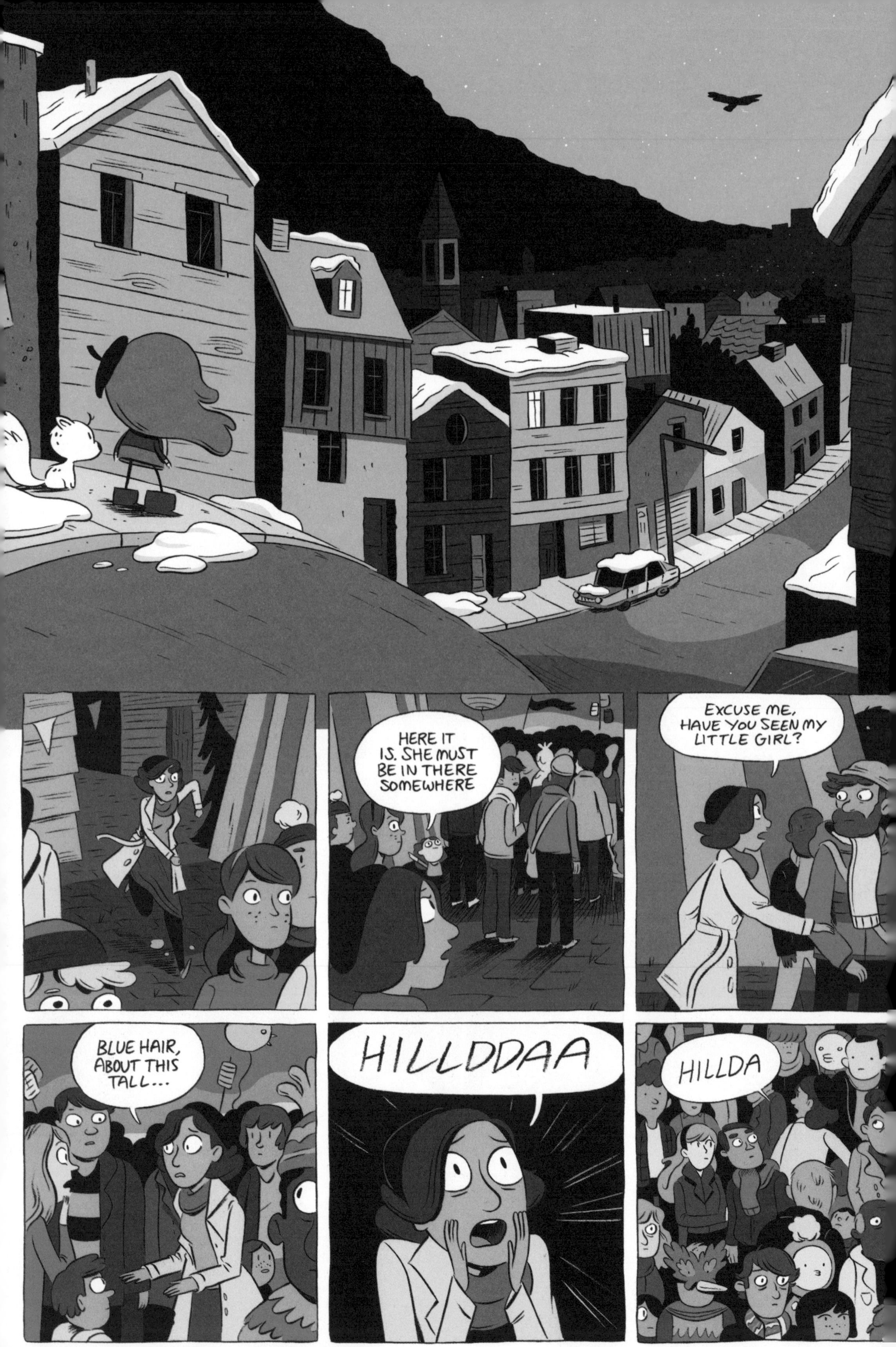

HERE IT IS. SHE MUST BE IN THERE SOMEWHERE
EXCUSE ME, HAVE YOU SEEN MY LITTLE GIRL?
BLUE HAIR, ABOUT THIS TALL...
HILLDDAA
HILLDA

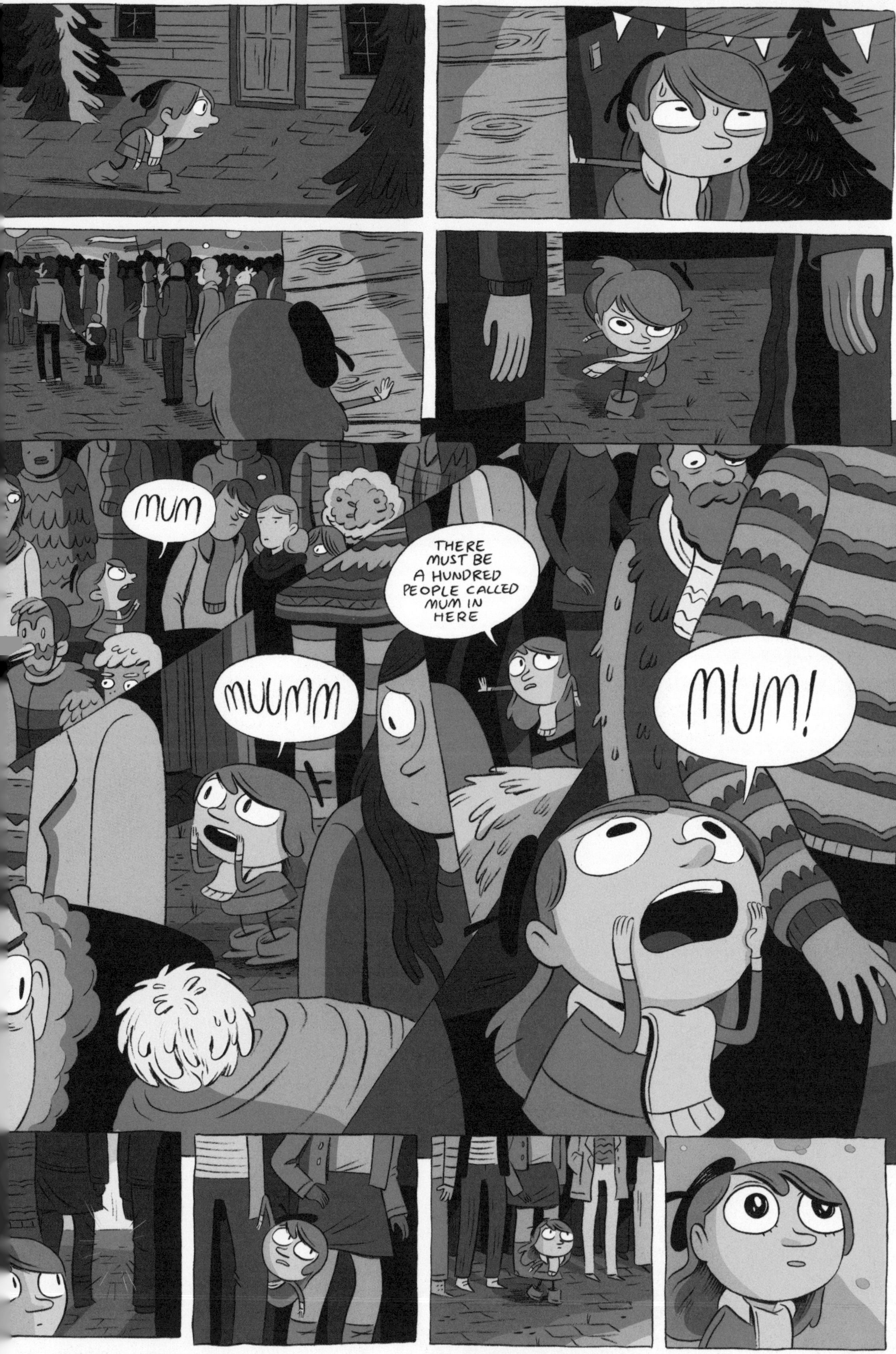
MUM
THERE MUST BE A HUNDRED PEOPLE CALLED MUM IN HERE
MUUMM
MUM!

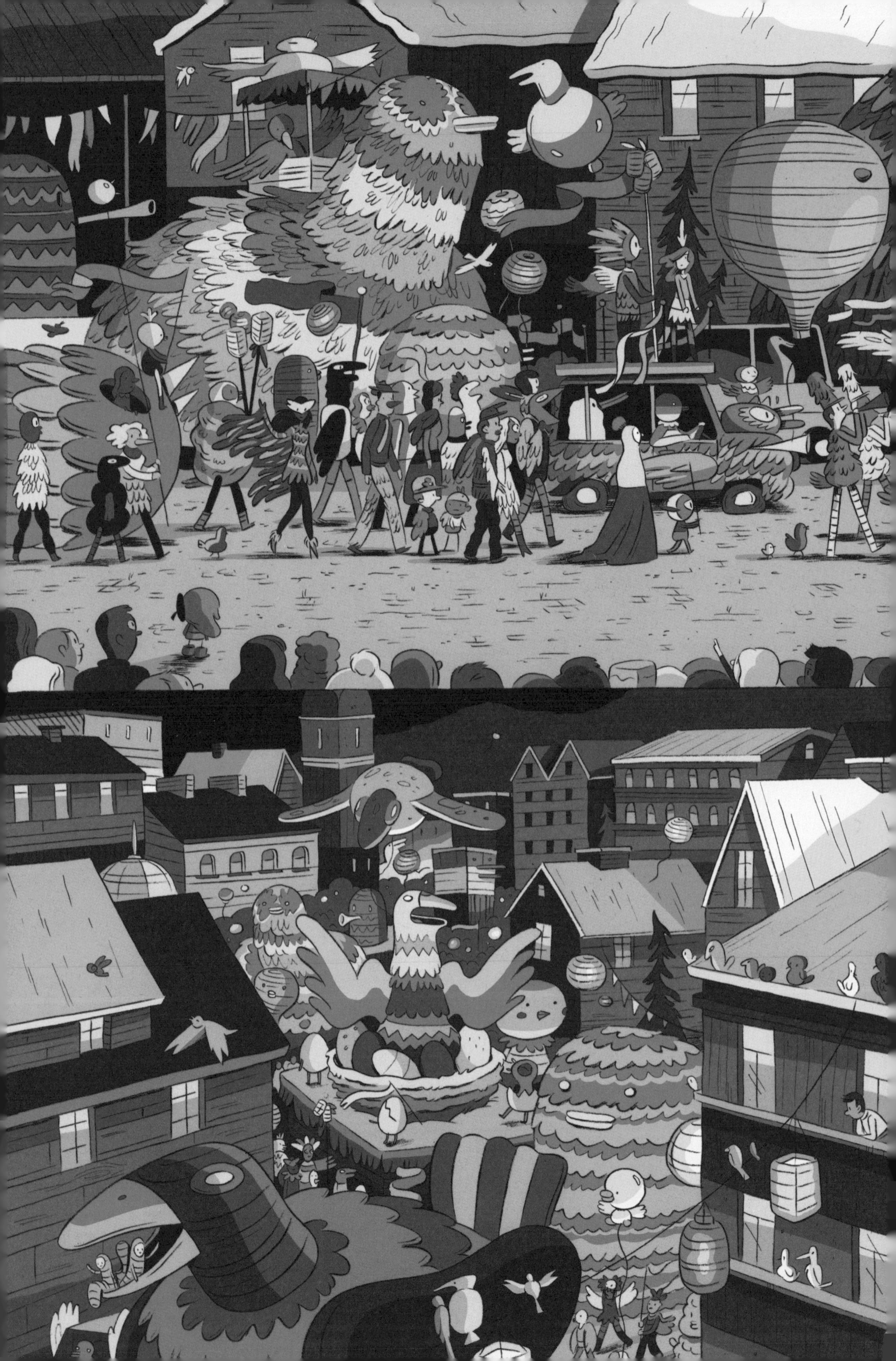

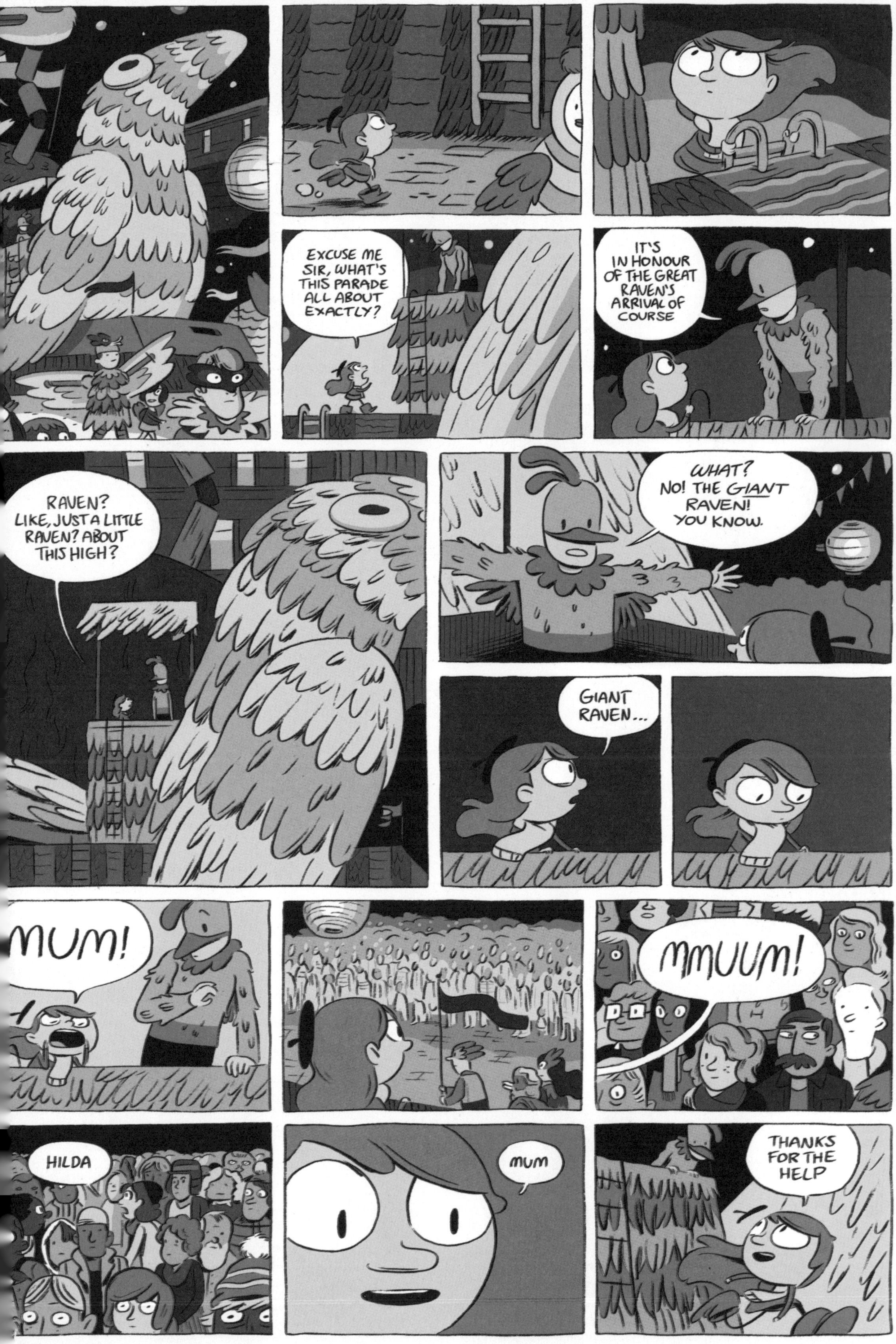
EXCUSE ME SIR, WHAT'S THIS PARADE ALL ABOUT EXACTLY?
IT'S IN HONOUR OF THE GREAT RAVEN'S ARRIVAL OF COURSE
RAVEN? LIKE, JUST A LITTLE RAVEN? ABOUT THIS HIGH?
WHAT? NO! THE GIANT RAVEN! YOU KNOW.
GIANT RAVEN...
MUM!
MMUUM!
HILDA
MUM
THANKS FOR THE HELP

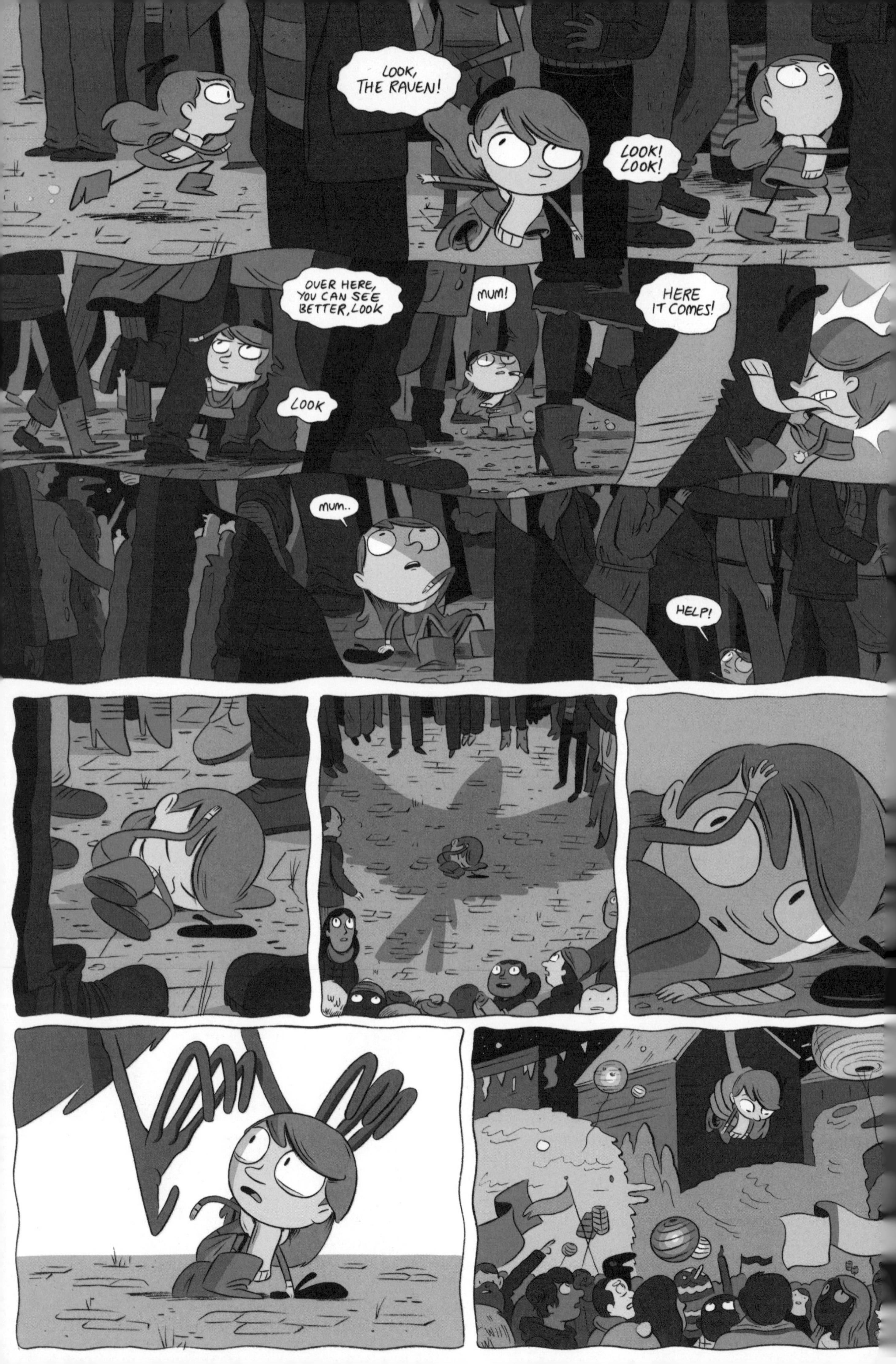
LOOK,
THE RAVEN!
LOOK!
LOOK!
OVER HERE,
YOU CAN SEE
BETTER, LOOK
MUM!
HERE
IT COMES!
LOOK
MUM..
HELP!

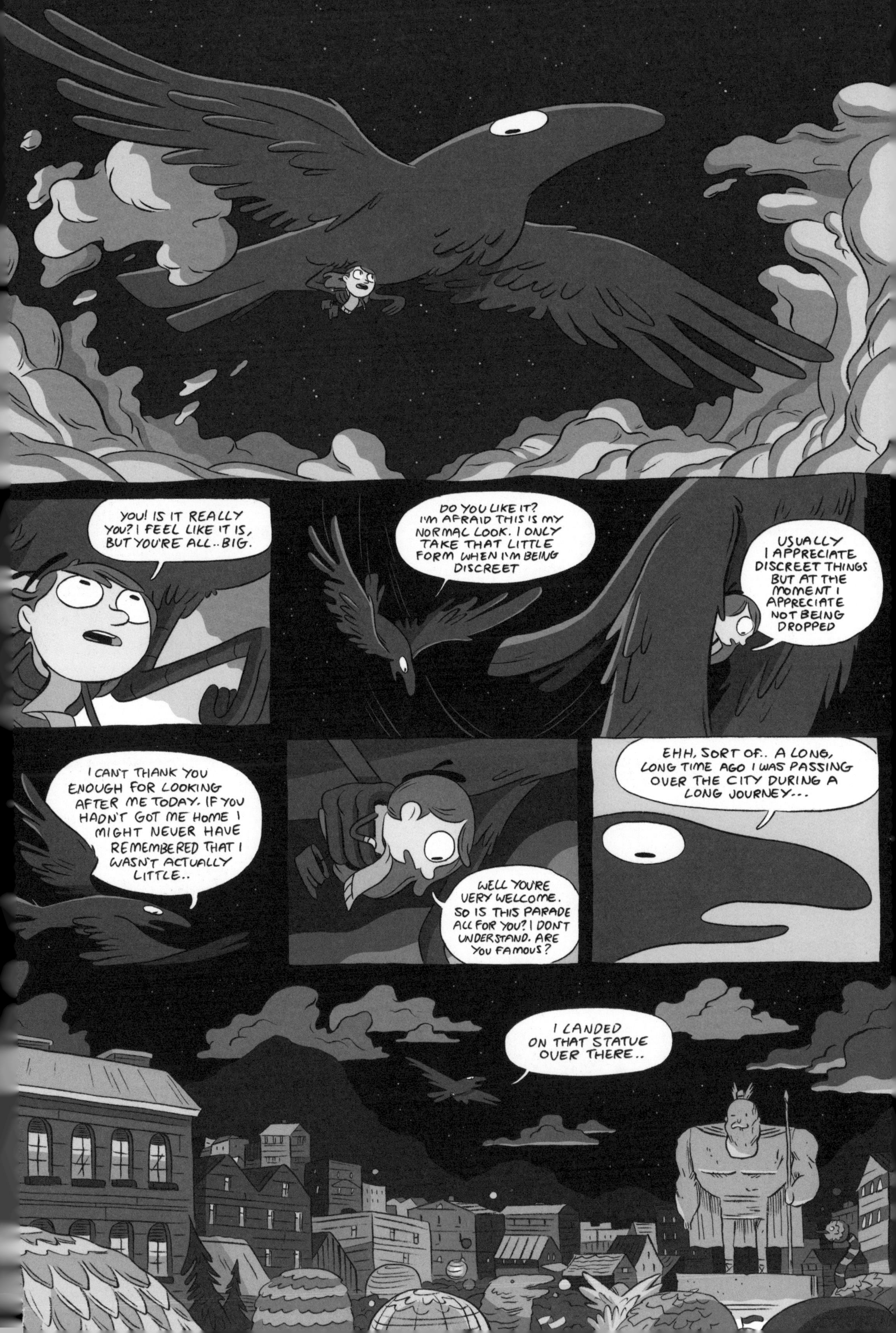
YOU! IS IT REALLY YOU? I FEEL LIKE IT IS, BUT YOU'RE ALL.. BIG.
DO YOU LIKE IT? I'M AFRAID THIS IS MY NORMAL LOOK. I ONLY TAKE THAT LITTLE FORM WHEN I'M BEING DISCREET
USUALLY I APPRECIATE DISCREET THINGS BUT AT THE MOMENT I APPRECIATE NOT BEING DROPPED
I CAN'T THANK YOU ENOUGH FOR LOOKING AFTER ME TODAY. IF YOU HADN'T GOT ME HOME I MIGHT NEVER HAVE REMEMBERED THAT I WASN'T ACTUALLY LITTLE..
WELL YOU'RE VERY WELCOME. SO IS THIS PARADE ALL FOR YOU? I DON'T UNDERSTAND. ARE YOU FAMOUS?
EHH, SORT OF.. A LONG, LONG TIME AGO I WAS PASSING OVER THE CITY DURING A LONG JOURNEY...
I LANDED ON THAT STATUE OVER THERE..

THE PEOPLE THOUGHT I WAS THE RAVEN MESSENGER OF THE GOD THEY WORSHIPPED

SENT TO SEE WHAT THEY WERE UP TO AND REPORT BACK TO MY MASTER.

IT TURNS OUT THE NEXT YEAR THERE WAS A GREAT HARVEST, GOOD WEATHER AND EVERYONE PROSPERED

THEY THOUGHT IT WAS M DOING! I PASSED THE NEX YEAR TO FIND A BIG FESTIV BEING HELD IN MY HONOU

THE YEAR AFTER, THEY THREW THE SAME PARTY. BUT I WAS OFF SOMEWHERE ELSE. PROBABLY AT HOME.

ANYWAY, THEY THOUGHT THEY'D DISPLEASED ME AND AS IT HAPPENS, THE NEXT YEAR WASN'T SO GREAT.

THERE WAS A SICKNESS, POOR CROPS AND THE COLDEST WINTER IN DECADES.

OF COURSE IT HAD NOTHING DO WITH ME! BUT FROM THE ON I DECIDED TO MAKE TH EFFORT TO SHOW MYSELF EVERY YEAR.

IF PEOPLE ARE EXPECTING AND ASSUMING THE WORST, THEY'LL GO OUT OF THEIR WAY TO SEE THE SIGNS OF IT.

AND WHO'D WANT TO MISS THEIR OWN PARTY? SO YOU'RE NOT A RAVEN GOD THEN? WHO ARE YOU?

I'M A THUNDERBIRD

WHAT'S A THUNDERBIRD

JUST A BIRD FOR THE MOST PART BUT I CAN DO THIS...

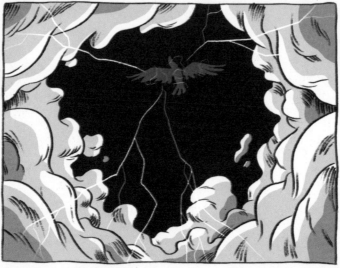

THEY SEEM TO LIKE THAT

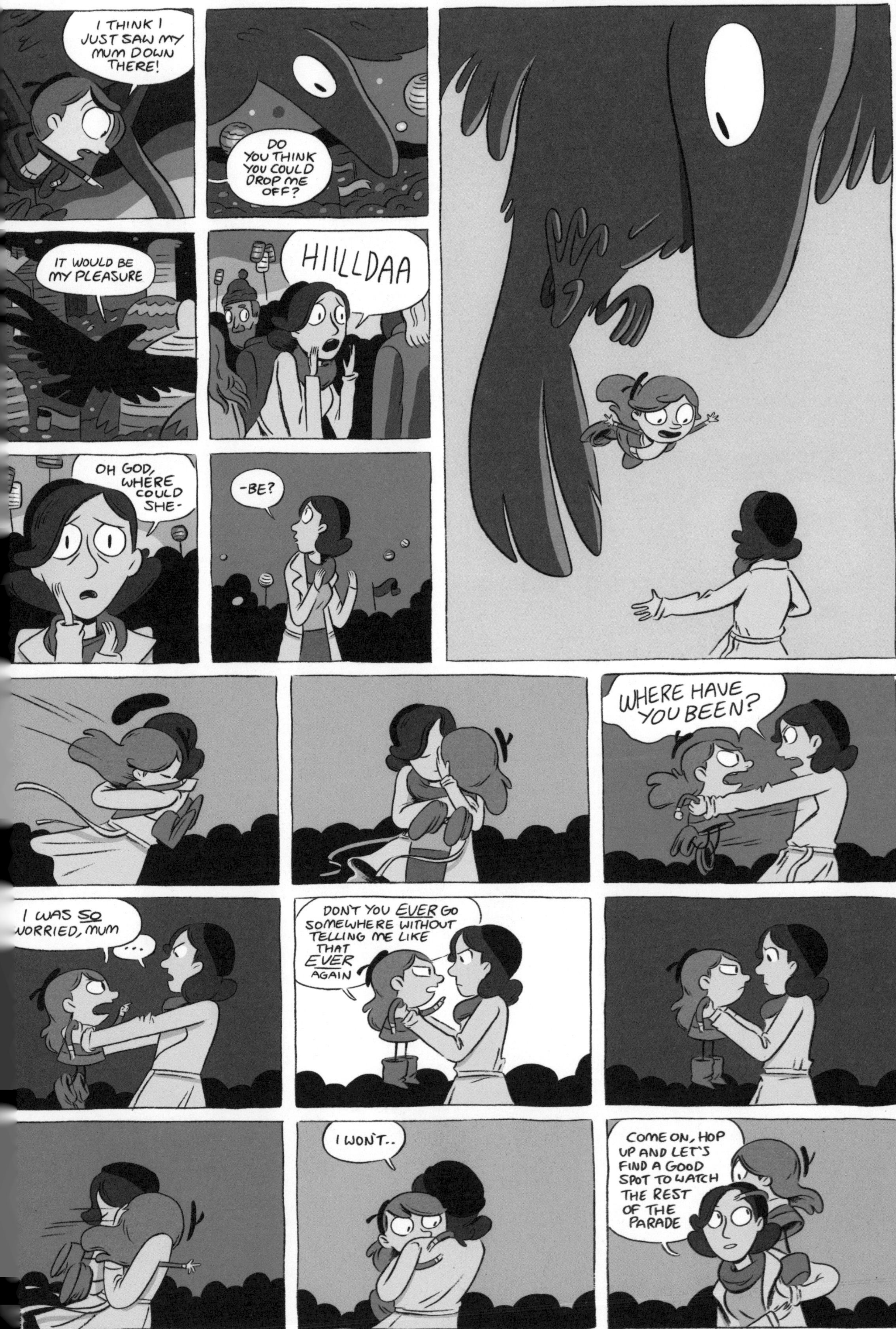
I THINK I JUST SAW MY MUM DOWN THERE!
DO YOU THINK YOU COULD DROP ME OFF?
IT WOULD BE MY PLEASURE
HIILLDAA
OH GOD, WHERE COULD SHE-
-BE?
WHERE HAVE YOU BEEN?
I WAS SO WORRIED, MUM
...
DON'T YOU EVER GO SOMEWHERE WITHOUT TELLING ME LIKE THAT EVER AGAIN
I WON'T..
COME ON, HOP UP AND LET'S FIND A GOOD SPOT TO WATCH THE REST OF THE PARADE

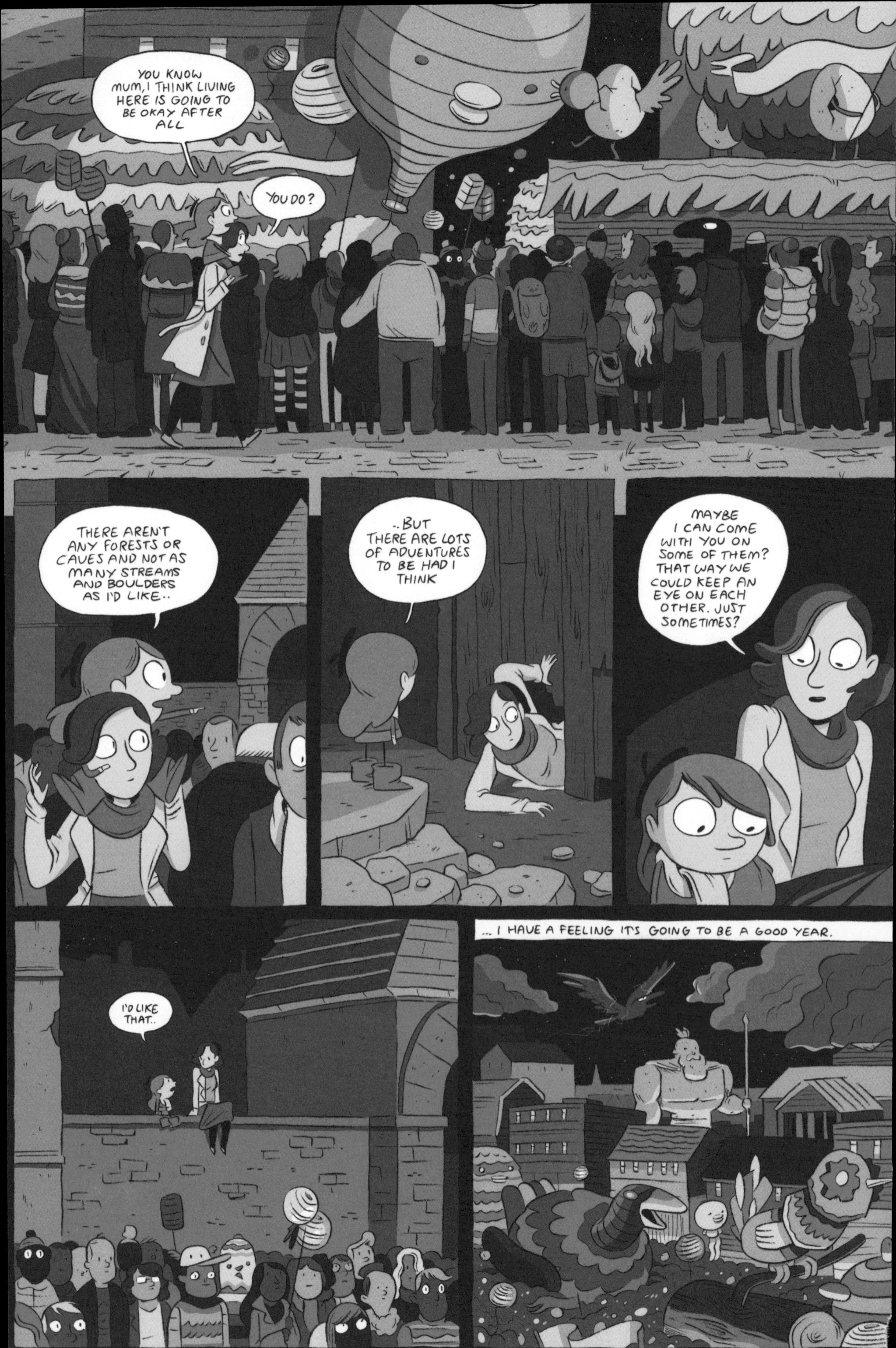
YOU KNOW MUM, I THINK LIVING HERE IS GOING TO BE OKAY AFTER ALL
YOU DO?
THERE AREN'T ANY FORESTS OR CAVES AND NOT AS MANY STREAMS AND BOULDERS AS I'D LIKE..
..BUT THERE ARE LOTS OF ADVENTURES TO BE HAD I THINK
MAYBE I CAN COME WITH YOU ON SOME OF THEM? THAT WAY WE COULD KEEP AN EYE ON EACH OTHER. JUST SOMETIMES?
I'D LIKE THAT..
... I HAVE A FEELING IT'S GOING TO BE A GOOD YEAR.

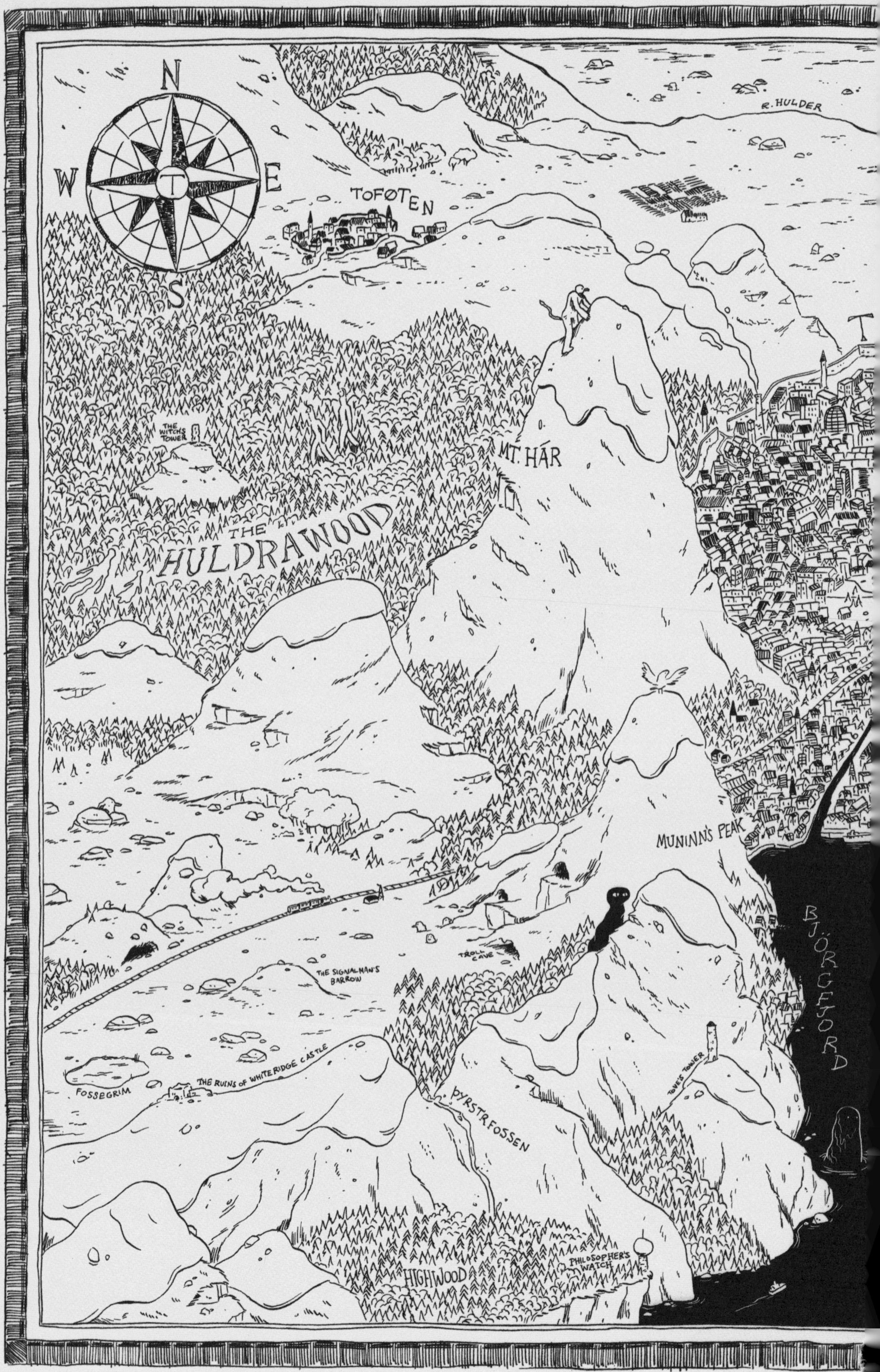
N
W
E
S
T
TOFØTEN
R. HULDER
T
THE WITCH'S TOWER
MT. HÁR
THE
HULDRAWOOD
MUNINN'S PEAK
TROLL CAVE
THE SIGNALMAN'S BARROW
BJÖRGFJORD
THE RUINS of WHITERIDGE CASTLE
FOSSEGRIM
ÞYRSTRFOSSEN
TOVE'S TOWER
PHILOSOPHER'S WATCH
HIGHWOOD

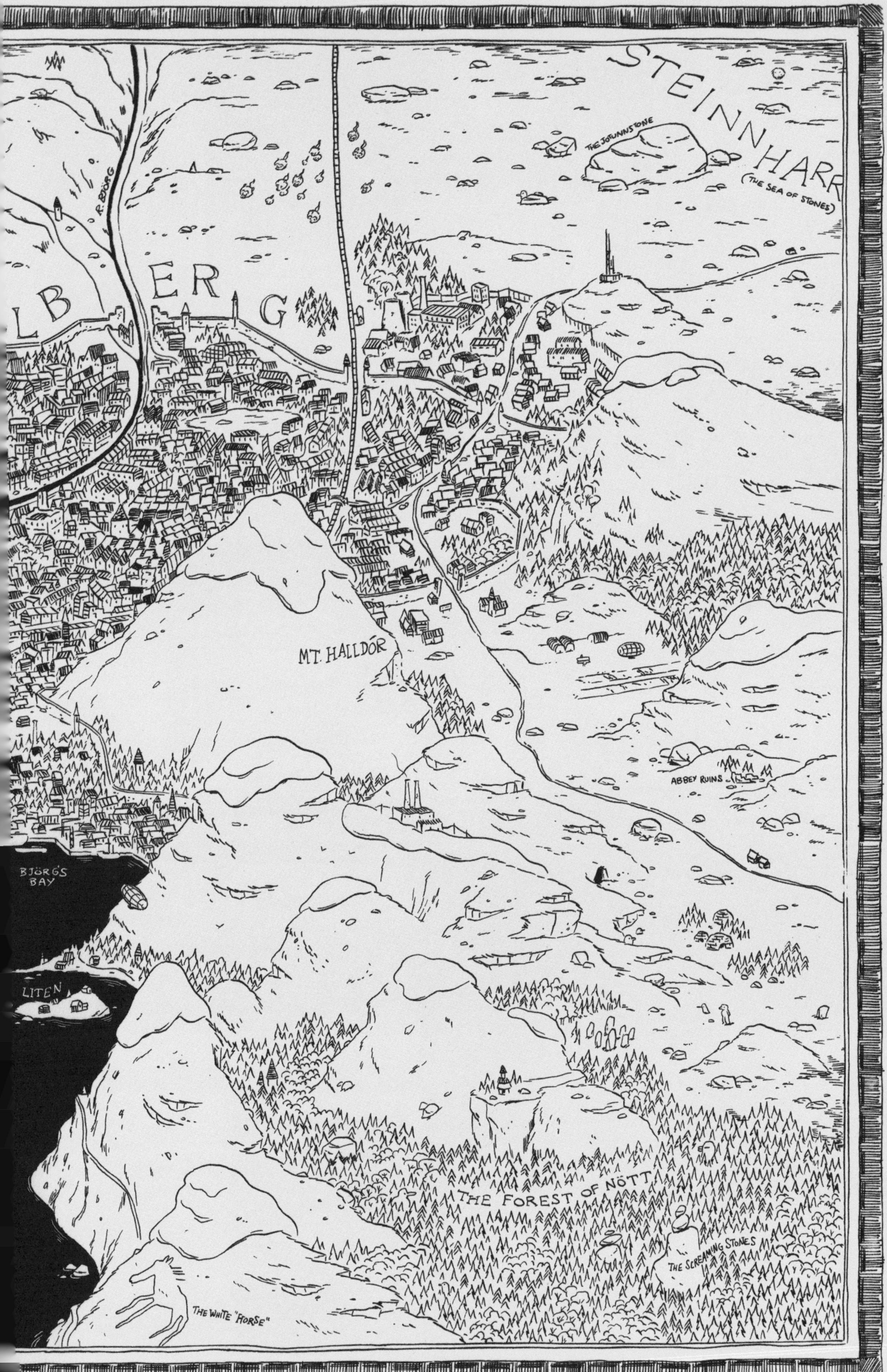

STEINNHARR
THE JOTUNNSTONE
(THE SEA OF STONES)
R. BJÖRG
LBERG
MT. HALLDÓR
ABBEY RUINS
BJÖRG'S BAY
LITEN
THE FOREST OF NÖTT
THE SCREAMING STONES
THE WHITE "HORSE"

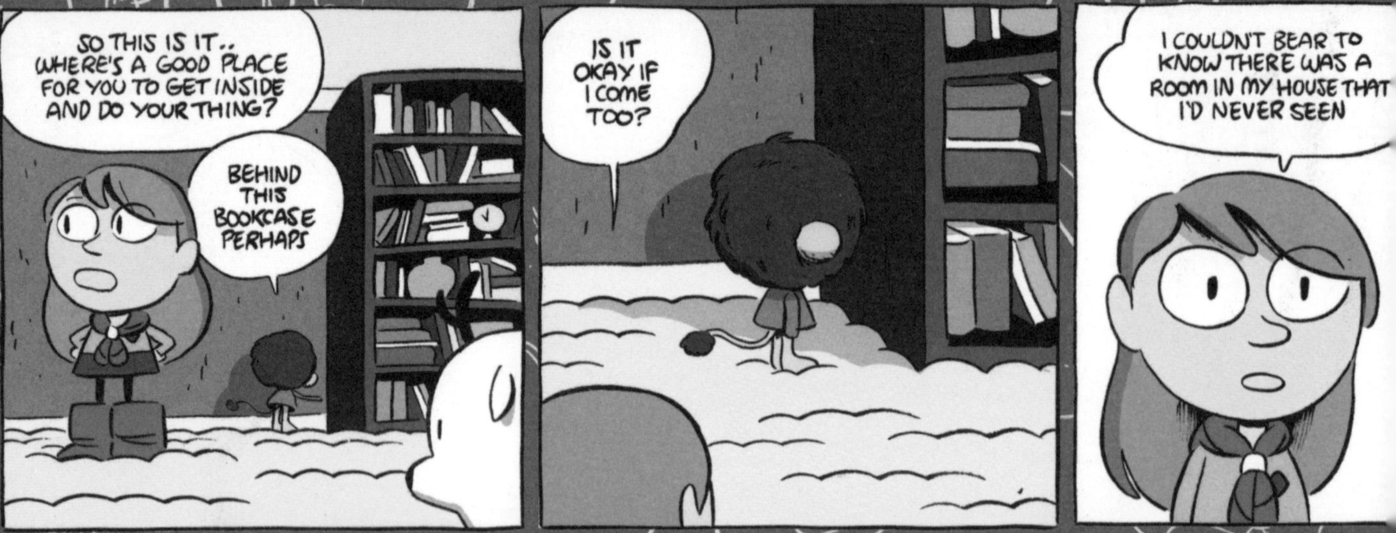
SO THIS IS IT.. WHERE'S A GOOD PLACE FOR YOU TO GET INSIDE AND DO YOUR THING?
BEHIND THIS BOOKCASE PERHAPS
IS IT OKAY IF I COME TOO?
I COULDN'T BEAR TO KNOW THERE WAS A ROOM IN MY HOUSE THAT I'D NEVER SEEN

IN HILDA'S NEXT ADVENTURE

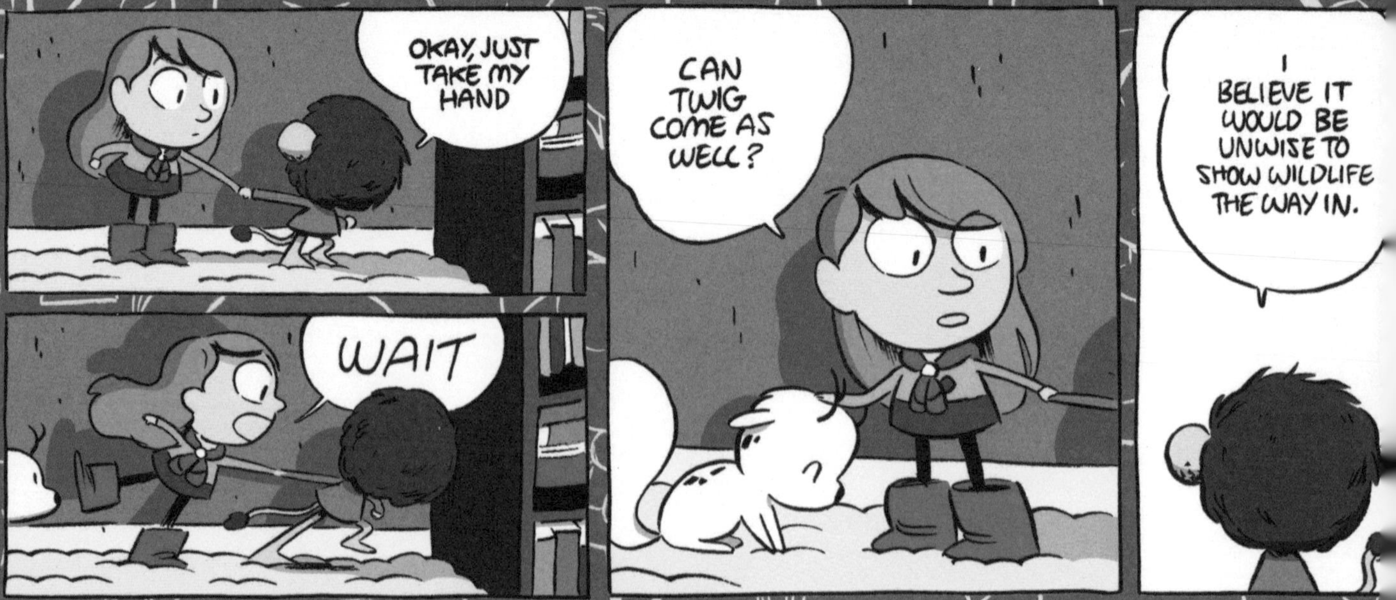
OKAY, JUST TAKE MY HAND
WAIT
CAN TWIG COME AS WELL?
I BELIEVE IT WOULD BE UNWISE TO SHOW WILDLIFE THE WAY IN.

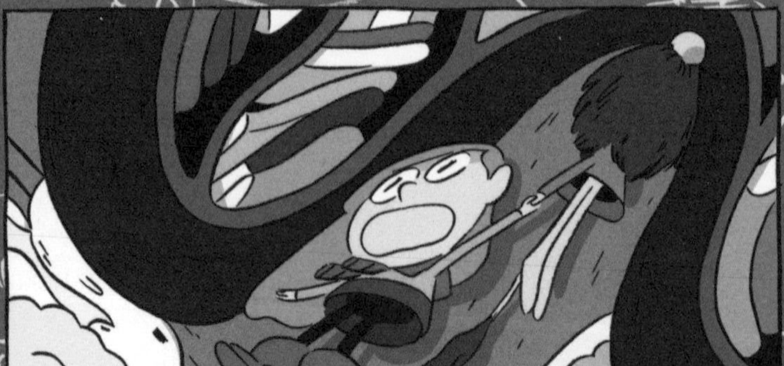

HILDA STUMBLES UPON TONTU, A LOST HOUSE SPIRIT. PLUNGED INTO THE SECRET WORLD OF THE NISSE, HILDA DISCOVERS HIDDEN PASSAGES THAT ONLY THE HOUSE SPIRITS CAN NAVIGATE... AND SOMETHING HAS BEEN RANSACKING THEM ALL!

WILL TONTU FIND HIS TRUE HOME?
AND COULD THIS ALL BE LINKED TO REPORTS OF AN ELUSIVE BEAST HAUNTING THE CITY?

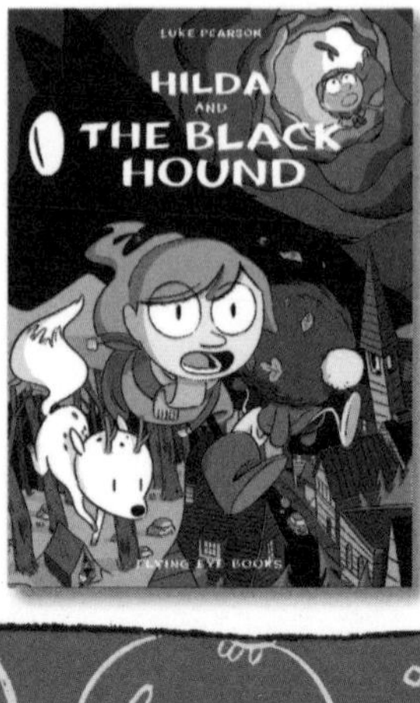
LUKE PEARSON
HILDA AND THE BLACK HOUND
FLYING EYE BOOKS

HILDA AND THE BLACK HOUND

ORDER FROM WWW.FLYINGEYEBOOKS.COM OR ALL GOOD BOOKSHOPS